Other Books by
Janet Tashjian

The Marty Frye, Private Eye series:

The Case of the Missing Action Figure
The Case of the Stolen Poodle
The Case of the Busted Video Games

The Einstein the Class Hamster series:

Einstein the Class Hamster
Einstein the Class Hamster and the Very Real Game Show
Einstein the Class Hamster Saves the Library

The Sticker Girl series:

Sticker Girl
Sticker Girl Rules the School

The My Life series:

My Life as a Book
My Life as a Stuntboy
My Life as a Cartoonist
My Life as a Joke
My Life as a Gamer
My Life as a Ninja
My Life as a Youtuber

Multiple Choice
Tru Confessions

Janet Tashjian

Sticker Girl
and the Cupcake Challenge

with illustrations by
Inga Wilmink

Christy Ottaviano Books

henry holt and company ★ new york

Henry Holt and Company, *Publishers since 1866*
Henry Holt® is a registered trademark of Macmillan Publishing Group, LLC
175 Fifth Avenue, New York, NY 10010 • mackids.com

ISBN 978-1-250-19647-7
Library of Congress Control Number 2018936459

Our books may be purchased in bulk for promotional, educational,
or business use. Please contact your local bookseller or the Macmillan
Corporate and Premium Sales Department at (800) 221-7945 ext. 5442 or
by e-mail at MacmillanSpecialMarkets@macmillan.com.

First edition, 2018 / Designed by April Ward and Rebecca Syracuse
Printed in the United States of America by
LSC Communications, Harrisonburg, Virginia

1 3 5 7 9 10 8 6 4 2

To Callie

Here we go Again!

It's only been a week since my last batch of stickers returned to their sheet and now Bev and I just found ANOTHER sticker sheet in the pocket of my dad's suitcase.

"You think they'd at least give me a few more days to get back to normal," I tell Bev. But the look on her face tells me she doesn't share my concern.

Bev puts a hand on my shoulder. "I've got news for you, Martina. This IS the new normal."

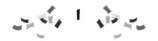

As exciting as these magical stickers have made my life—I would never have become BFFs with Bev without them—the last batch caused a lot of trouble, and I'm not really ready for that much adventure yet.

Bev, on the other hand, is ALWAYS ready. (I guess it's easier to be carefree when the stickers aren't yours.)

"I know you want to peel off Craig first," she says.

Every sheet of magical stickers I've found has included Craig, a grumpy little cupcake I've gotten used to having around.

"Look at what ELSE is in here!" I point to the cell phone that was just ringing and that led us to the suitcase in the back of the garage. This phone was on my LAST sheet. Why did it come back?

"Maybe it's a bonus sticker," Bev says. "Like at the smoothie

shop—when you buy
enough smoothies,
they give you
one for free."

I reach into
the suitcase to
grab the magic
phone, but when
I look down it's
GONE.

Bev and I lock eyes and I know she just felt
the same sinking feeling in her stomach that I
did. I gaze at the old sheet of stickers in my hand.

"Phew!" I exhale. The cell phone is now safely
back on the older sheet with the other stickers.
The last thing I need is a runaway sticker wreak-
ing magical havoc all over town.

Bev grabs the old sheet from my hand. "What
would happen if we peeled off two Craigs at once?
Can you imagine TWO talking cupcakes?"

I can't. Craig is quite opinionated for a cupcake,
and one of him is pretty much all I can handle.

I put the old sticker sheet back in my closet. I make sure to pile some books and board games on top of it—just in case these stickers feel like pulling any more funny business.

With that last sheet secure, I feel better about taking out the new one. These are my magical stickers this time:

- Craig (of course)

- lipstick

- ant farm

- calculator

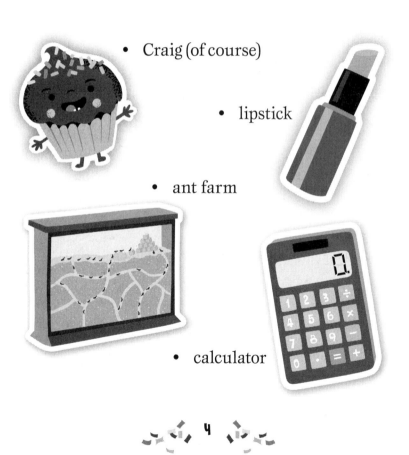

- beaded bracelet

- gumball-machine robot

- two adorable kittens

- ice cream cone

- baseball bat

- wave

5

With my other magical stickers, I tried to plan when I used them, spacing them out to maximize the magic. But Bev is bouncing up and down on her heels, itching to start using the stickers today. If it were up to her, we'd peel off every one of them NOW.

"How about the kittens?" she asks. "They're so cute—I can't stand it!"

Bev's right—bringing the kittens to life is definitely appealing, but I know which sticker I have to choose first.

I slowly peel off Craig, my buttercream-covered friend.

whoosh! poof! Bam!

In a puff of glitter and confetti, Craig suddenly appears in my hand. He makes a big to-do, hacking up tiny pieces of glitter. "It's always such a fuss," Craig complains. "Why does GLITTER have to be involved? Aren't stickers that come to life and talk enough?"

Bev and I smile at our favorite pastry pal.

"You're such a grouch," I tell him. "But I still missed you. Even though you've only been gone a week."

I can't say for sure because of the sprinkles, but it looks like Craig just smiled.

"Are you ready to have some fun?" he asks.

I just hope the fun doesn't come with so much trouble this time.

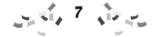

A new plan for our class

Bev's mom texts her to come home for dinner, but Bev's on a mission to peel off the sticker of the kittens. I promise to wait until we're together again before releasing the cute pets; Bev's not having it, though. I'm just as anxious to see the kittens as she is, but I remember how much work the puppies were on my first sheet, so I have to be cautious.

"Everyone wants kittens! Everyone wants puppies! Everyone wants unicorns!" Craig says. "What about good old-fashioned baked goods?"

Craig's rant gives me an idea.

"Remember how you two talked me into running for student council president?" I ask them.

"As I recall, we had to volunteer FOR you," Craig says. "You never would've run for that position on your own."

"We've been going back and forth about what kind of fund-raiser to have and I know bake sales aren't that original . . ."

"TOTALLY," Bev and Craig say in unison.

"But we have a spokesperson now!" I gesture toward Craig.

"Oh, am I supposed to lure people to the sale with my cupcake batter—I mean, banter?"

Bev laughs. "You ARE pretty chatty for a cupcake."

"Flattery will get you everywhere," Craig says.

At our last student council meeting, Mike, Scott, Samantha, and I tried to decide what kind

of event we should have to raise money for our school library. Now that he's back, why not use Craig to advertise our sale on the school website or even on YouTube? Cupcakes are so popular these days; there's even a famous bakery in Beverly Hills that has its own show on YouTube called *Cupcake Challenge*. Bev and I watch their web series all the time.

Mom's only taken me to get a treat there a couple of times since the line is always wrapped around the block. Their cupcakes are so incredible that they installed a cupcake ATM outside the shop. People can buy a perfectly boxed, tasty cupcake right from the machine. There's usually a long line for that too.

"*Cupcake CHALLENGE!?*" Craig nearly leaves his buttercream behind when he hears us talking about it.

I hope we're not making too much noise because I'd like to avoid the *Where did you get a talking cupcake?* conversation with my parents for as long as possible.

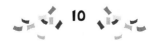

"You don't mean a fight-to-the-death challenge, do you?" Craig asks.

Bev laughs. "It's a baking show with kids from all across the country competing for first prize."

I can't believe Craig hasn't heard us talking about *Cupcake Challenge* before. Craig picks up a paper clip from the desk and starts lifting it as if it's a barbell. "It's very sedentary when you're stuck on a sheet of stickers," he says. "I need to move." He does several reps with the paper clip. "Besides, if I'm going to help advertise your bake sale, I've got to get ready for my close-up!"

I've never really understood how time works in the sticker world. Craig was only

11

back on his sheet for a week in human time. I ask him how long it felt on his end.

"Let's just say it was enough time for my legs to fall asleep." He starts doing karate kicks.

I want to press him for more information on what happens when he and the other stickers return to the sheet, but Bev's mom is out front to pick her up.

"Promise you won't unleash the kittens till we're together," Bev says. "Don't peel off the lipstick sticker either."

I tell her I wouldn't think of it.

Once she's gone, I try to start on my homework, but it's no use.

I HAVE MAGICAL STICKERS AGAIN!

An Odd Bracelet

Bev asked me to save the kittens and lipstick but she didn't say anything about the rest of the stickers. I can hear Mom and Dad yelling at the basketball game on TV, so the coast is probably clear. I decide to pick the sticker that will need the least amount of explaining to my parents. After some internal debate, I choose the bracelet.

whoosh! poof! Bam!

The beautiful

bracelet

suddenly appears in my hand. The beads look like they're made of shiny blue glass, with white circles and black dots on each bead. I slip it around my wrist; it's by far the nicest piece of jewelry I own.

"Why are you staring at it?" Craig asks. "Are you waiting for it to start talking?"

I hate that a cupcake knows me this well.

"YOU talk," I answer. "Why can't a bracelet talk too?"

"My guess is that you'll be waiting quite a while." Craig hops onto my bed and points to Mom's laptop. "How about some YouTube? I really missed watching videos and I'm dying to see what this cupcake show is all about."

I tell Craig we're not watching *Cupcake Challenge* right now because it's impossible to watch just one episode. The kids on that show are insanely creative and the tasks are unbelievable. I've seen them make things like enchanted gummy-bear cupcake forests and cupcake volcanoes that erupt Fruity Pebbles. And for a breakfast challenge, one kid even baked maple-bacon cupcakes and topped them all with sunny-side-up eggs. If we start watching now, I'll never get my homework done before dinner. My abuelita is coming over tonight and I want to have time to hang out with her.

"All right, all right," Craig says. "I'll watch something else."

I can't prove my grandmother has had anything to do with my magical stickers but I still can't escape the nagging feeling that she does. When my father brought home my first sheet of magical stickers as a present from a business trip, it turned out that the woman who owned the store he got them from was a friend of my abuelita's. The mysterious store owner insisted Dad get them for me and then wouldn't take his money. Family friends call my grandmother *la bruja*, which means "witch," because she used to tell fortunes around the neighborhood that often came true. To me, she's just my feisty, quirky abuelita.

I finish the last problem on my worksheet just in time to help Mom set the table. She's training a new colleague at the insurance office where she works this month, so she's busier than usual. We're both people who deal with extra work by being even more organized, so there are to-do lists and sticky notes all over the house reminding Mom about her hair appointment and not to forget to pay the cable bill by Sunday. The flurry of activity when Mom's crossing things off her lists might make other people nervous, but it always makes me feel like the world is manageable and she's in control.

"Marti—please fill the water glasses and make sure James has washed his hands."

My guess is that the kid with the dirtiest hands in our family is my sixteen-year-old-brother, not the two-year-old, but I drag James to the sink just in case. He grabs the dishwashing brush and pretends he's brushing his teeth, wearing a huge grin as the soapy bubbles fall onto the floor. My older brother, Eric, used to be this much fun, but since he started high school his sense of humor is turned on only when he's with his friends or a girl he wants to impress.

Dad comes into the house with my abuelita. She may be old, but she has eyes like a hawk. She immediately spots my new bracelet.

"Ohhhhhh," she whispers. *"Un hechizo."*

When I ask her what she means, she gently takes my wrist and points to the black dot inside the white circle in the center of the bead. "This is a special bracelet."

You're telling me. It was a sticker half an hour ago.

"These beads ward off *la maldad*—the evil eye."

My mother removes her apron and hugs my grandmother. "She needs to learn about fractions," Mom says. "Not the spirit world."

"I WANT to know about it," I say. Maybe the spirit world can help explain why I keep finding sheets of magical stickers.

"This bracelet can ward off evil," my abuelita continues. "Not that anyone would ever cast a spell on a smart, beautiful girl like Martina Rivera! La presidente of her class!"

Even though I won the student council election a while ago, my grandmother finds a way to bring it up each time she sees me.

"The only spells in this house are the ones your mother cast over this delicious dinner," Dad says. "Let's eat."

It's hard not to notice how many new gray hairs Dad got after we moved to the San Fernando Valley. Back in San Diego, his hair was jet black, but since he bought the diner here, the salt in his hair has definitely overtaken the pepper.

Mom serves the carnitas straight from the slow cooker, where it was simmering all day. Eric races into the house. He's still wearing his white shirt and apron from his job at the coffee shop and grabs the last bowl from the counter before taking a seat. Eric may mess up a lot of things around the house, but he's smart enough to know not to miss dinner when our grandmother's here. Mom shoots him a look to slow down and stop slurping his carnitas.

Everyone's listening to Eric's story about a guy who came in for coffee with a cockatoo on his shoulder and how the bird got loose and flew around the shop, but the only thing I'm focused on is my new bracelet. Does it really have the power to keep evil at bay? Are there people walking around in this day and age casting spells? Is warding off evil something I need to start worrying about?

As if to answer my questions, my abuelita nods with her eyes fixed on my bracelet. We make eye contact and she smiles. *Could she hear what I was thinking?!*

When she opens her mouth to speak, it isn't about my bracelet or evil spirits. "Looks like we've got a young artist in the family." She laughs and motions over to James. As usual, the tablecloth at James's end of the table is covered with more food than made it into his stomach.

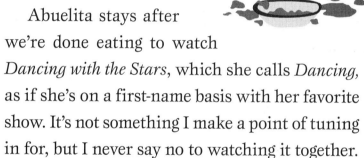

Abuelita stays after we're done eating to watch *Dancing with the Stars,* which she calls *Dancing,* as if she's on a first-name basis with her favorite show. It's not something I make a point of tuning in for, but I never say no to watching it together.

My abuelita is on the edge of her seat and I smile at how she can be as excited as a toddler trying to catch bubbles for the first time. Even if she had nothing to do with my stickers, she still is one of my favorite people in the world, hands down.

I'm helping Mom pick up the kitchen when my abuelita comes in to say goodbye. She has her driver's license but Dad and my aunts usually prefer to drive her, especially at night.

"Buenas noches." She kisses me on the forehead and holds my wrist one more time. She closes her eyes and talks under her breath as her fingers encircle the bracelet. When she opens her eyes, she lets go of my hand with a clap. "No more talk of evil spirits. This bracelet now brings only good luck."

She winks at me on her way out the door.

Is there something my abuelita isn't telling me about my stickers?

student council

All Bev wants to talk about in school on Monday is my new sheet of stickers. Her parents took her family on a mini-vacation to Santa Barbara for the weekend so it's been two whole days since she's seen the new sheet.

The rest of my weekend, on the other hand, was far from relaxing. After working a few extra hours at my dad's diner, I stayed up late reading everything I could find online about magic charm bracelets. I ask Bev what she thinks the dots on my bracelet mean but she's too focused on the kittens.

"I think we should definitely peel them off next," she says. "But a robot might also be cool—especially if it can help with chores. I'd do anything to get out of emptying the dishwasher every night."

Even though I agree, I'm more anxious about the student council meeting and if the others will like my ideas for the bake sale.

The other night after my abuelita left, I begged Craig to help me market my bake sale idea. "No one cares about bake sales," he said.

"But they DO care about cupcakes. After all, they're everyone's favorite treat." My comment was meant to butter him up—that's a cupcake joke—and it did. Craig spent the next half hour helping me make a short video that I'll present to my friends on student council today.

When the final bell rings, I head to the multi-purpose room for our meeting.

"I'm coming to your house after you're done," Bev calls to me from her locker. "It's sticker time!"

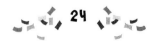

At the meeting, Mike's got a stack of papers in front of him and for a moment I feel like I'm not organized enough. Then I realize it's a stack of comic books and breathe a sigh of relief. (I hate not being the most prepared person in the room. ANY room.)

The president is supposed to start the meetings but Samantha, our secretary, always likes to, which is fine with me. Even though my stickers have gotten me into several situations I've had to talk myself out of, I'm still most comfortable hiding in the back of the room, staying quiet and trying not to be noticed.

We talk about how well the new cubbies are working out and how the reading loft needs new pillows. After Nancy got the flu and threw up all over them last week, no one wants to use them, even after Ms. Graham took them home and washed them. "But the biggest thing we want to raise money for is getting some new books for the library."

Scott, who is the treasurer, tells us we don't have much money left.

"Martina, do you still think a bake sale is the way to go?" he asks.

"It has to be Bake Sale 2.0," Mike says. "Nobody wants the same old congo bars and Rice Krispies treats."

"Speak for yourself," Scott says.

I take Mom's laptop from my bag and hold it for the others to see. "I made a commercial over the weekend to show you how we can reboot the typical bake sale."

When I hit PLAY, Craig fills the screen, staring straight into the camera. His expression is mean, like a cupcake tough guy. "You want a piece of me?" he asks. "Well, do you?" He's holding out his fists like he's ready to fight, but then smiles into the camera. "OF COURSE you want a piece of me," he says. "I'm a CUPCAKE! Come on down to the elementary school this Friday and pick up your favorite treat! See you then!"

What I don't tell the others is that this

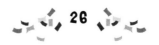

ten seconds' worth of footage took eighteen takes because Craig couldn't get his lines down. (Cupcakes might be fun to hang out with but they're terrible at memorizing lines. I finally had to agree to let Craig improvise and quote old movies.)

"This is great!" Mike says. "We can put it on the school website and have Ms. Graham do an e-mail blast to all the parents and share it on the social media sites."

"We can start signing people up tomorrow," Samantha adds. "Make a list of who's bringing what so it's not all chocolate chip cookies."

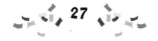

"Not that there's anything wrong with that," Scott says.

"You did a great job, Martina. But how did you animate that cupcake?" Mike asks. "It looks pretty real."

I make up a story about Eric helping me with the animation software he has on his computer.

"I'm getting into video editing too," Mike continues. "I could come over and help make more videos to generate buzz for the sale."

I hate lying but I tell him that Eric is picky about letting other people use his computer. "I'll do the videos," I say. "Do you want to help recruit volunteers?"

Mike is really nice and making commercials for the sale with him would be fun, but I can't risk letting anyone else but Bev know I've got a real talking cupcake living in a plastic container in my room.

Dad picks me up at school after the meeting and, sure enough, the second I walk in the door, Bev appears.

"Before we get into any new stickers, I have some presidential duties to attend to," I tell her.

We hurry to see if Ms. Graham uploaded Craig's bake sale commercial to the school's social media accounts. She did, and Bev nearly falls off the edge of the bed from laughing when she sees Craig's tough-guy act.

"Martina, this is HILARIOUS," she says. "You have to tell Ms. Graham to tag *Cupcake Challenge* on these!"

Bev's idea is a great one. Getting a like or a comment from our favorite web series would be a nice accomplishment for our class—not to mention the publicity it could get our school. Maybe they'll even give us a shout-out on the next episode.

I leave comments on all the posts tagging Cupcake Challenge. Bev leans over my shoulder. "We should also tag the host too and double the chances of it getting seen by the right people—especially Christy Morales."

"Since when did you become such a hashtag expert?" I ask.

"My mom does this for a living, remember?" Bev answers. We fist-bump and Bev heads to my bag to pull out the sticker sheet.

"Come on, Sticker Girl," she says. "I know two kittens just dying to come out and play."

meow

Bev doesn't realize that there can be disastrous side effects when you bring a sticker to life. Never mind the whole magic thing, there are several reasons keeping kittens in the house could get me in trouble. First off, Eric hates cats. Second, how do I explain them to my parents? But the BIGGEST problem is how I'm going to introduce them to Lily, my Chihuahua. She's been more than patient with Craig and with Walter the chipmunk ballerina; cats, however, are a different thing altogether. Whenever Mr. Rutledge's

Siamese cat, Queenie, sneaks out of their house down the street, Lily doesn't stop barking at the window until Queenie goes back inside. The barking will be 24/7 with two kittens living here.

To be safe, I rummage through the garage and dig out the small crate we used to train Lily and bring it inside my room. Lily's not too happy about losing her freedom, so I coax her inside the crate with her favorite salmon treats.

Bev hands me the sheet of stickers from my desk and asks if I'm ready. She might explode if I keep these kittens from her any longer.

whoosh! POOF! BaM!

Two of the cutest

KiTTens

suddenly appear in my room. Bev and I have to control ourselves not to squeal with excitement.

Lily barks from inside her crate. I try to calm her down while Bev frames the kittens with her mom's phone and takes a photo.

"Don't be fooled," Craig says. "They may seem tame, but they're wildcats! I've lived with them on that sheet—I should know."

"But they're such sweeties!" Bev sits next to

me on my bed. "What filter do you think I should use to take a photo of them?"

We scroll through a few filter options until Lily starts barking like crazy.

I rush over to my faithful Chihuahua and pick her up from the crate. "What's wrong, girl?"

"Uhhh, Martina," Bev says, "where did the kittens go?"

We look under the bed, in the closet, and even in a few dresser drawers. The kittens are gone.

So is my sheet of magic stickers!

come out, come out, wherever you are

"I told you those kittens were trouble," Craig says.

"Why didn't you stop them?" I ask him.

"I didn't realize I was supposed to do everything around here," he answers.

"Do you think Lily can track their scent?" Bev asks. She holds out her sweater where one of the kittens was lying. It doesn't take long before my dog is hot on their trail.

Lily races out of the room with Bev and me close behind her. We slow down when we reach the kitchen, where Dad is preparing fish for dinner.

"Looks like Lily's in a hurry to get outside." Dad laughs. "You're cleaning up any accidents, not me."

I hope the smell from the fish doesn't throw Lily off track.

When I open the door to the backyard, Lily runs outside and heads straight to James's turtle-shaped sandbox, where the two kittens are working together to fill buckets with sand. I scoop up Lily to avoid a nasty confrontation.

"Are they . . . ?" Bev's sentence trails off.

We watch in disbelief as the two kittens add turrets to the giant castle they've built in the middle of the sandbox. It looks like it was modeled on the Sleeping Beauty Castle at Disneyland.

"Did those kittens just MAKE that?" I ask. "And where is my sheet of stickers?"

Bev points at the bottom of the castle. "I

think that's a moat and your stickers are the drawbridge."

Sure enough, the sticker sheet is neatly placed over the trough of water.

"Don't ruin my magic stickers!" I yell.

When the kittens carry the buckets over to the hose to fill them up, I yank my sticker sheet out of the sandbox.

"What kind of kittens are they?" Bev asks. "Michelangelo couldn't have sculpted a better castle."

"I have no idea," I reply. "I just hope they weren't trying to drown the rest of the stickers."

I'm suddenly knocked off my feet by my little brother running from the other side of the yard. Nothing makes James happier than building things in his sandbox, although his lop-sided creations could never compare with the kittens' masterpiece. Without stopping to appreciate the details of such an exquisite sculpture, he dive-bombs the sandbox, destroying the castle and sending the kittens scurrying across the grass. I guess I grabbed my magic sheet of stickers just in time.

"Play with cats!" James says. "I want cats!"

James struggles to reach the two kittens, who are now grooming themselves under the swing set. I bend down to calm him.

"What should we call the kittens?" I ask him. "Do YOU want to name them?"

James's face lights up. "Burger and Fries!"

His random response makes Bev and me smile. I ask James which kitten is which.

He points to the dark one and proclaims her Burger.

"I guess that makes the other one Fries," Bev says, laughing.

Dad comes outside to tell us dinner's ready. He knows how much Bev likes his cooking, so he asks if she wants to stay. She calls her dad before he's finished asking.

"And where did these two come from?"

Uh-oh. Dad noticed the cats, though he doesn't seem affected by their cuteness the way Bev and I were. "You've got to be careful with strays," he says. "They can be feral."

"These kittens aren't feral, Mr. Rivera." I can always count on Bev to come up with explanations for my stickers. "I'm cat-sitting them for a few days."

I guess that makes it official—the kittens are now staying with Bev.

"Then I guess it's a good thing we're having fish." My father gestures for us to come inside but the mischievous kittens have already beat us to it.

I head in, hoping these kittens will behave.

A
CUPCAKE
DiVa

Burger and Fries love the scraps of fish Dad puts in bowls for them to eat. Mom and Eric are still at work so it's easy for Bev and me to steer the conversation away from the kittens and keep it on school and the diner.

Dad seems a little sad when he tells us that business has slowed down. We moved to the San Fernando Valley so Dad could buy this diner, but with the bad economy and local food competition, he's not doing as well as he thought he'd be.

"Making good food isn't enough anymore." He sighs. "People care more about how their food looks now than how it tastes. Why does everyone have to take pictures of their meal before they eat it?"

"Your food looks good AND tastes good," Bev tells him. "You make the best pancakes and your nachos are insane!"

Dad smiles. Nothing makes him happier than people enjoying his food. The fish we're eating now has been sautéed in garlic, onion, tomatoes, capers, and green olives. They're all simple ingredients but my father has a unique way of cooking them so they taste incredible.

After dinner, James reaches out with greasy fingers and begs Dad to read to him. He's obsessed with a new picture book about trucks and Dad's happy to oblige, which means Bev and I are free to play with the kittens.

But the kittens are no longer in the kitchen.

"I'm beginning to get suspicious of those felines," I whisper to Bev.

"Cats always get into crazy situations," she tells me. "It's what makes them so popular on the internet."

We race to my room, where Burger and Fries have Craig pinned to the wall.

"I told you these cats couldn't be trusted!" Craig yells. "They're trying to eat me!"

Bev scoops up Burger while I take Fries.

"Cats don't eat sweets," I tell Craig. "They're pretty much carnivores."

Bev shakes her head. "You are such a nerd sometimes, Martina. I love that you know such random facts!"

When you spend your life being the most timid kid in class, there's lots of extra time to study information about cats or ducks or turtles. (There's also lots of time to play with stickers.) Of course none of this helps Craig, who is now in the middle of a full-blown panic attack.

"It's either me or them!" he says, and points. "I can't relax with these monsters here!"

Bev and I can't help but laugh at our dramatic cupcake friend.

"Careful, Craig," Bev says. "I think your buttercream is boiling."

I pick up Craig and put him on the dresser. "I know you're upset, but you have to admit two tiny kittens holding a cupcake hostage is pretty funny."

"Get them out of here!" Craig flails his arms and legs.

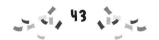

"I really can take the kittens home—my mom will love them," Bev says. "The last thing we need is a stressed-out dessert."

"But it's going to cost you," I tell Craig. "You have to help me shoot a few more commercials for the bake sale."

Craig crosses his arms. "Only if I get final cut."

"You're the most demanding cupcake EVER," I say, laughing. "You'll only get final cut if you stop complaining. Otherwise I'm going to keep the kittens here forever."

Bev holds Burger and Fries toward Craig to emphasize my point. Craig backs away quietly as Bev's dad beeps the horn outside.

"Just because you have a magic sheet of stickers doesn't mean you have to use every single one," Craig tells me after Bev leaves. "You might be better off without some of them."

"What if I'd left YOU on the sheet?" I tease.

"I'm not talking about me!" Craig answers. "Who knows about that robot or those ants!

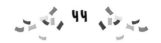

Either one of those stickers might try to destroy the world!"

Craig's over-the-top personality is starting to get on my nerves so I take out my notebook with ideas for some new videos to advertise the bake sale. My plan had been to collaborate with Craig on some of the sketches but it might be time to put on the director's hat and tell him what I need him to do instead. Maybe being president of my class IS helping with my leadership skills.

It takes a while to get Craig calm enough to be camera ready, so I ask Dad if I can borrow his phone. After a few vocal exercises, Craig is set to go. Although when we shot the test commercial it took many tries for Craig to get his lines right, this time he's on a roll and does most of the commercials in one take. I think being frightened out of his frosting might've been just the motivation he needed.

We film for less than an hour but Craig's exhausted. He collapses onto my pillow like Cleopatra. I'm glad Lily's snuggled on the couch with Dad and James because Craig looks pretty edible right now.

"You're not going to ask me to sing and dance at the bake sale, are you?" he asks.

"I wish there was a way you COULD. People would flock to our table if they saw a singing cupcake." When the Pegasus sticker came to life, I told my classmates it was animatronic; there's no chance the same story would work again to explain Craig.

I wipe away some stray crumbs and lie down on the bed next to Craig. Despite all the complaining, he's been a huge help. "You did a great job with the videos. Our school will be able to buy lots of new books thanks to you."

"Speaking of books . . ." Craig gestures to the backpack on the foot of the bed.

I was so busy with Bev, the kittens, and the videos that I forgot to do my homework.

"If you're thinking about peeling off the robot to do it for you, forget it," Craig says.

Of course, that's EXACTLY what I was thinking. Can ALL cupcakes read minds?

A robot who does homework would be amazing, but I can't take that chance.

I grab my science book and take notes on solids, liquids, and gases as I fight off yawns. Sometimes being Sticker Girl is exhausting.

All systems go

Mike, Samantha, and Scott LOVE the new clips of Craig. When we show Ms. Graham, she leans back in her swivel chair and puts her hand over her mouth.

"Martina, these are so cute," she says. "You might have a real future in animation!"

"I do animation too," Mike adds.

"I had no idea you kids were so talented," Ms. Graham gushes.

I quietly thank Ms. Graham for the compliment, but I know I don't really deserve it. I never doubted that Craig's confectionery charisma would be a huge hit with the student council—he was practically made to be in front of a camera—though I wish I didn't have to lie about how he really moved across the screen. I've now accidentally convinced my teacher that I'm some kind of cartoon-creating whiz kid when Mike's the real filmmaker. Suppose Ms. Graham asks me to animate something in front of the class and I have no idea what to do? Will she and my classmates think I'm a fraud? Is it bad to take a shortcut in my work if I'm lucky enough to have magical stickers? I'm honestly not sure I would've been elected class president without a whole lot of sticker magic.

I'm so distracted by my thoughts that I miss the discussion the others are having with Ms. Graham about the details of the bake sale.

"What do you think, Martina?" Samantha asks.

Does it look like I'm not paying attention? Will Ms. Graham think I don't care?

"Do you think thirty kids bringing baked goods will be enough?" Samantha hands me a list of what all the families have committed to bringing. I realize I spent so much time making videos that I forgot to go to the school website and sign up to bring something for the sale.

I take the clipboard from Samantha and add my name to the list.

"I suppose you're bringing cupcakes," Mike says. "You're so good at animating them, baking them will be a piece of cake!"

Everyone laughs at Mike's joke. I hope he isn't upset with me for not letting him help with the animation.

When the bell rings, we take our seats and Ms. Graham hands each row a stack of papers to pass back.

"Clear your desks. We'll begin today with your vocab quiz."

When the test gets to me, I immediately regret spending so much time last night chasing after

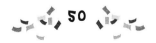

Burger and Fries. I barely know half the words on the quiz.

Most of my classmates are already attacking these definitions but I'm still on the first word.

"You have ten minutes to finish," Ms. Graham says. She gives me a small smile as I stare into space so I turn my eyes back to my paper.

I'm usually a stellar student—not because I love being a teacher's pet but because I can't stand being caught off guard. It was easy to stay on top of my assignments and even read a few chapters ahead when I was the shy new girl in school. Having friends and student council responsibilities— not to mention a whole world of magical stickers to keep under control—

doesn't leave me nearly enough time to prepare the way I used to.

"Pencils down." Ms. Graham stands at the front of the room to collect the papers.

I've never handed in an incomplete quiz before; I feel so guilty that I spend the rest of the day taking pages of notes and listening intently to all my teachers.

After school, Samantha and I wait for rides together. It turns out she also likes to watch *Dancing with the Stars,* so we discuss which couple we think will win. Samantha has been taking ballet classes for years and stands straighter than any kid I know. Waiting in front of the school with her makes me adjust my posture too.

When Eric picks me up, I get in the car as gracefully as I can, hoping some of Samantha's ballet discipline will rub off on me.

"What are you doing?" my brother asks. "You look stiff as a board."

I ignore him but find myself slouching into my seat within minutes.

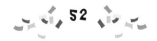

"Dad wants us to swing by the diner," Eric says. "Debbie called to say she couldn't work for him anymore, so he needs some help."

"Debbie's leaving?!" Debbie is our favorite waitress, and she's been with our family since Dad first bought the diner. She taught Eric and me little tricks to save time and keep customers happy—like cleaning ink from an exploding pen off your hands with a lemon wedge and always having crayons handy for families with kids. Debbie takes college classes at night and worked in the diner four days a week. She has tattoos of Japanese fans on both her arms and can remember most people's orders without writing them down. I always thought of her as the older sister I never had. If losing her is hard on me, I can't imagine how devastated Dad must be.

"Business is really slow, so Debbie didn't have a choice. She wasn't earning enough in tips to make ends meet," Eric continues.

Last time I was at the diner, Debbie didn't complain about how little she made in tips that morning, but I could tell she was used to making more.

"What's she going to do now?" I ask. "I hope we still get to see her."

"I'm taking her to the movies on Saturday," Eric says. "So I definitely will."

My mouth hangs open in disbelief. Eric fake-punches me in the arm to let me know he's kidding.

"Debbie would never go on a date with you— even to the movies, where no one could see her."

"Very funny." Eric turns his head to look in the other lane so I can't see his smile. That's how it is with Eric now—hiding his feelings pretty much all the time. I don't want to be like that when I'M in high school.

When we get to the diner, Dad looks tired but I'm sure some of that is sadness from Debbie quitting. I act extra happy and ask him to help me bake cupcakes for the sale on Friday.

He tells me he'd love to help but I can tell his

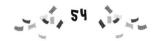

mind is focused on how he's going to manage with one less worker. Debbie was a pro who easily did the work of two servers; it'll be difficult to find someone to replace her.

Eric has a research paper due tomorrow so he can't stay long. Dad tells me to fill all the napkin dispensers and condiment bottles while he and Eric go to the back room to take stock of what needs to be ordered.

I've been helping Dad with side work around the restaurant for so long that you'd think I'd have these chores done in a flash, but no matter how many times I stack the napkin dispenser, one of the napkins always ends up sticking out from the pile and I have to start all over again.

Only fourteen dispensers to go when the diner phone rings with a call from Bev.

At first I don't know what she's talking about when she mentions Burger and Fries. Then I realize she wants me to come over to play with the kittens. I tell her I'd love to be playing with

kittens instead of working here for the next few hours and she responds with one word: STICKERS.

Of course! I've got a robot right here in my backpack! Even if the robot has some weird hobby like the ballerina chipmunk or zombie DJ from my last sheet, it's still a ROBOT. It's got to be better at these repetitive tasks than I am.

The problem—as always—is how to explain the sudden appearance of something strange and new—in this case, an android at the diner. This robot's head IS a gumball machine; maybe I can say I got us a free trial of the Gumball Machine of the Future to put by the cash register.

I smile to myself and whisk the sticker off the page.

whoosh! Poof! Bam!

"A little rough there, weren't you?" When the robot rubs his head with his metallic hand, a

yellow gumball falls out of his mouth and onto the floor.

"Don't even think about eating that," he tells me. "Unless you want to spit out your pancreas for ME to chew on."

"Gross! No!" I hand him back the gumball and he takes off the top of his glass head and pops it back in with the others.

I ask him why he's talking with a British accent.

"It's the only one I've got. I'm from England."

I want to ask how a British robot sticker landed on a sheet my dad got in California but I can hear my dad and brother in the back room and have to make up a story—fast.

Dad and Eric swing through the doors and stop short when they see the robot. Before I can come up with a believable story, the robot greets them.

"Hello, I'm Model M29," he says. "But you can call me Nigel. I'm here to help."

Eric looks at me with an expression of utter confusion but Dad just points to the ketchup bottles lined up on the counter and tells Nigel he can start with them.

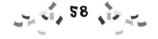

"Uh . . . where did the robot come from, Martina?" Eric can't stop staring at Nigel, who's already filled two bottles of ketchup without spilling a drop.

His question must wake Dad out of his worry daze because he's suddenly interested in the answer too.

"It's a funny story," I begin. *Why did I listen to Bev? I'm not good at coming up with explanations like she is!*

"I'm part of the new robotics lab at Martina's school," Nigel interjects.

"I went to that school too," Eric says, "and there's no robotics lab."

"There is now!" I point to Nigel, who's already moved on to the mustard. "Nigel's been programmed to do all kinds of things."

Eric's still not buying it. "What kind of things?"

Nigel stops working. "I follow instructions to the letter. My résumé is quite extensive, if you must know."

"Nigel's been helping all the kids in my class," I add. "I've been so busy with student council, I forgot to tell you it was my turn to take him home."

Eric circles Nigel with a raised eyebrow. "I drove you home from school and there definitely was NOT a robot in the car."

"Yeah . . ." My voice trails off. I notice a delivery truck leaving the store across the street. "The last kid who took him home just dropped him off."

"Seems like Nigel knows his way around a restaurant," he says.

"He does!" I cross my arms and turn to Eric. "Don't get any ideas about Nigel filling in at the coffee shop," I say. "He's working with just me and my class."

Dad must still be flustered from losing Debbie. "I'll take all the help I can get, even from a gumball machine," he says.

"I BEG YOUR PARDON," Nigel says. "I am a mechanical being of the highest intelligence."

Dad smiles. "You're certainly better than the cotton-candy machine I bought last year. That thing was impossible to clean. You can help out anytime."

Dad takes Eric back to the walk-in fridge to record inventory of the meats and dairy. I thank Nigel for making up the story about the robotics lab.

"It isn't a story," Nigel says. "I've dispatched electronic mail to your principal and student council members with my blueprints to begin work immediately."

What?!

Nigel's gumballs bounce around inside his head and he shoots me a look that, if he were human, could only be described as a smirk. "I'm not sure you have anything to say about it, Martina."

Who's in charge here—me or the robot?

I get to Bake!

It's dark by the time we get home from the diner. Dad apologized several times for having me stay so late, but there was no one else to help him. Usually the diner closes at nine o'clock, but tonight business was so slow Dad closed an hour early. The optimist in me wants to believe he locked up early because I was there, but I see how much it upsets him to stand at the counter and watch people walk past the diner and into the trendy restaurants down the street.

We bring home some unsold chicken fajitas

to make a quick dinner for him and Mom. Dad asks Nigel if he wants to sleep on the couch but Nigel laughs and explains that sleep means something different to a robot. He then plugs himself into the hallway outlet and wheels into the hall closet alongside the mop and broom. It seems like an uncomfortable way to spend the night, but I'm too tired to argue. I collapse onto my bed.

When I check on Nigel the next morning, he's no longer in the closet but folding laundry alongside Mom.

"Nigel was just telling me about the new robotics lab," Mom says. "I miss one PTO meeting and suddenly your school is zooming into the future!"

She hands me a glass of orange juice and spoons out some scrambled eggs from the skillet. Eric comes into the kitchen and takes a forkful of eggs off my plate until Mom hits his hand with the wooden spoon and he gets his own.

"I thought your school was broke," Eric says. "You're having a bake sale to buy books but you have a robotics lab? Doesn't make sense."

I'm surprised Eric was actually listening at dinner the other night when I talked about the sale. Before I can answer, Nigel does.

"EVERY school should have a robotics lab. Robots are the way of the future!" He neatly folds one of James's shirts and puts it on top of the tidiest pile of laundry I've ever seen.

"That doesn't really answer my question." Eric sinks his teeth into a piece of toast.

"Well, if the robots that come out of the new lab are half as helpful as Nigel, then let the fundraising begin!" Mom hands me the folded clothes to drop off in our rooms but Nigel intercepts and whisks the stacks down the hall.

"I could really get used to having him around," Mom says. "How long before you have to pass him on to the next student?"

"Uhm, he's mine for a few more days at least," I answer. "But don't get too attached." I

run upstairs before Mom or Eric can ask any more questions.

As much as I love having a houseguest to help with chores, I worry about what kind of ruckus Nigel's planning on causing at school. After I finish brushing my teeth, I find him waiting by the front door, eager to tag along.

"I must say, I cannot WAIT to get started on this new adventure."

Nigel's been so helpful, but he must have a few wires loose if he thinks I'm taking him to school—today or any day.

"I need you to stay here and help me prepare," I tell him. "I've got to bake cupcakes for the sale."

Gumballs swirl around inside Nigel's head. "Gathering ingredients, mixing, then baking one dozen cupcakes requires forty-seven minutes," Nigel answers. "I certainly don't need all day."

Nigel's organizational skills make me look like an amateur.

"Besides," I continue, "my father needs you at the diner."

Dad walks over with his keys, ready to drive me to school. "I would LOVE an extra pair of hands at the diner today—you're a godsend, Nigel."

"Finally, someone who gives me the respect I deserve." Nigel swivels around and follows Dad to the car, itching to get to work. I can see I'm going to have to come up with a giant family to-do list to keep Nigel busy and distract him from the robotics lab idea.

The school day passes pretty quickly, thanks to an assembly on fire prevention. Bev keeps leaning over during the visiting firefighter's speech and asking me questions about Nigel. "What part of England is he from? How is he going to build a robotics lab? You left him alone with your dad all day?!" Another teacher finally comes over and makes Bev switch seats with a girl on the other side of the room.

The assembly is a great opportunity to turn off my brain and just listen, but as the firefighter finishes, I know it's time to get back to my to-do list. First and foremost, I've got to crank out some cupcakes for tomorrow's sale.

When I get home, I'm shocked to see HUN-DREDS of cupcakes covering every surface of the kitchen—counters, table, even the top of the fridge. The ones on the dining room table are stacked in a giant pyramid.

All the cupcakes have buttercream frosting and look exactly like Craig.

"This isn't funny!" screams a familiar voice.

I can tell it's Craig but I can't find him amid all the chocolate clones.

"OVER HERE! OVER HERE!"

I follow his voice to the middle of the cupcake pyramid and find him in the second row from the bottom.

I laugh. "You look good enough to eat."

"Here's a tip," Craig says. "If a robot ever asks if you want to be a model, say NO!"

I look over to Nigel, who's washing a mixing bowl, and tell him he did an amazing job. "But I thought you were helping Dad today?"

"I organized the stockroom, cleaned the oven and grill, recycled all the bent silverware, washed the baseboards, and waxed the floor. He brought me back home because there was nothing else to do."

I don't know how to tell Nigel I was actually

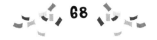

looking forward to baking tonight. I'm not a kid who just WATCHES cooking shows; I actually like to cook too. Bev was going to come over and help; will her mom still let her come over with the kittens if the baking's already done? How was Nigel supposed to know I wanted to bake those treats myself?

"If you don't get me out of here right this second," Craig says, "I'm going to sneeze and bring this whole thing down!" Poor Craig does seem uncomfortable in that pyramid.

I take apart the lavish display and rescue my cupcake friend.

"It's hard to feel special when there are others who look just as delicious as you are," Craig complains.

"At least you're the only one who talks," I say. As soon as the sentence is out of my mouth, I wonder if it's true.

I pick up a few different cupcakes. "Hello? Hello?"

"Why are you talking as if they can answer?" Nigel asks. "They just came out of the oven! They're cupcakes! Cupcakes that look delicious!"

Craig looks at me and sighs.

"Are you sure you don't mind?" I ask.

He rolls his eyes and tells me to go ahead.

I pull down the pleated liner and take a bite of the warm cupcake.

"Nigel—these are incredible!"

"You're welcome," Craig answers. "I'M the one who gave him the recipe."

I wonder how Craig knows what ingredients he's made out of. I certainly can't name all MY body parts.

It doesn't take more than a few bites to finish the cupcake. Even though the only others in the kitchen are Craig and a robot, I resist the temptation to lick the buttercream frosting off my fingers. It's one of the things that drives Mom crazy and she's burned into us to reach for a napkin instead.

When Mom gets home, I borrow her phone

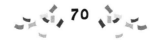

and snap a few photos of the kitchen full of cup-cakes. Mom then forwards them to Ms. Graham, who can post them on social media. Christy Morales and the *Cupcake Challenge* crew have GOT to see this!

If these cupcakes are any indication, tomor-row's bake sale is going to be a huge success.

The Bake Sale

In addition to moviemaking and cartoons, it turns out Mike is pretty good at organizing too. He scheduled two different times for the bake sale—one at morning drop-off and one at afternoon pickup. Our class is the only one doing the fund-raiser, so we'll be able to target every kid and parent during those two slots. Mike and I would probably make a great team if I didn't have to keep Craig and the other stickers a secret.

Samantha, Scott, and I divide the baked goods into morning foods—muffins and assorted breads and pastries—and afternoon treats—brownies, cookies, bars, and cupcakes. Mike and Samantha also set up cones in the parking lot to make sure people from the neighborhood can park and get goodies too.

Dad drives me to school forty-five minutes early. He offers to stop at our favorite donut shop to get me a hot cocoa and chocolate twist but I tell him I'm saving my appetite to buy something at the sale. He hands me a ten to get something for him and Mom and to "keep the change." Although my parents don't like to talk about it in front of us, I know they've been worried about money, so it means a lot to have Dad show his support for our class's efforts.

As I place two of Samantha's mom's cinnamon rolls into a paper bag for Dad, Scott comes over.

"I want to eat every single one of these."

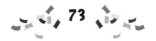

Scott's eyes are as glazed as the cinnamon rolls as he gestures to the three large tables displaying everything our class will hopefully sell. "Can the class treasurer also be the official taste tester?"

"You can definitely taste-test the quinoa date bars Noreen's mom made," Samantha says. "They look like they're filled with centipedes."

Seeing all the homemade goodies laid out, I can't help but be proud of our work. You can tell some items were made without much help from a grownup—like Scott's lopsided M&M cookies— but a few things look good enough to be in a bakery window. A few weeks ago this bake sale was just an idea in my head, but the whole class came together to make it happen. Maybe I'm a pretty good class president after all.

Mike holds up one of the Craig clones. "Martina, I don't think you made enough cupcakes," he jokes. "There's enough to feed three football teams, and our school doesn't even have a football team!"

Ms. Graham lays two crisp bills on the table for a blueberry muffin. "You kids have done a fantastic job. Not only does the food look great, the social media campaign you suggested was very effective. A woman at my gym told me she's stopping by because she saw the sale posted on Instagram."

While the others were busy orchestrating sign-ups and scheduling parking-lot shifts, I worked with Ms. Graham to make sure Craig's bake sale commercials were on the front page of the school website, sent as an e-mail blast to all parents, and posted on social media. It was exciting to watch people "like" the sale and pass the post along to friends.

Ms. Graham looks out the window to the cars lining up for drop-off. "After today, our school library will be able to afford LOTS of new books."

The rest of our class and the custodian help us set up the tables. Ms. Graham takes out the cash box we used at our last fund-raiser, as well as the scanner that lets her process credit cards on her phone.

Bev pulls me aside. "You're not going to believe this," she says, "but the kittens did some more artwork last night."

Bev carefully reaches for her bag and pulls out a model playground—complete with a slide and swing set—made entirely out of old soda cans and water bottles.

I can't believe my eyes. "The kittens MADE this?"

"I heard strange noises coming from our recycling bin," Bev says. "When I opened the lid, I found the kittens putting this together."

It's a pretty impressive model. Who knew these cats were such artists? Bev places the sculpture as the centerpiece on the largest table.

Suddenly, parents and kids are lining up to buy food and Scott is drowning in fistfuls of money. I tell Bev I'll see her in class and rush back to work.

The next hour is a blur of sugary treats and

cash. We sell out of the Neelys' muffins, and all that's left of the Habibis' rugelach is a few crumbs at the bottom of the aluminum pan. I can see Mike and Samantha stressing about the line of hungry customers eager to get on the road and I figure this is my chance to save the day. I've worked many busy Sundays at the diner and know how to handle multiple checks with a smile. All the parents are impressed with my professionalism and I regret not putting out a tip jar.

The morning bake sale is so popular that Mike, Scott, Samantha, and I get excused from our first class. I'm even more relieved because with all the commotion in preparing for the sale, I didn't have time to read the assigned chapter in our history textbook on the original thirteen colonies.

As we walk down the hallways on our way back to class, I'm elated with the success of the morning shift. Kids I don't even know are munching treats and waving. This might be the best school day I've ever had—until I open the

door to my classroom and see three words written on the chalkboard that bring my spirits crashing down.

SHOW-AND-TELL.

How did I let show-and-tell presentations slip my mind?! I don't know what's wrong with me lately. First an incomplete vocab quiz, and now I forgot an assignment?

I keep my head down and try not to be noticed as I take my seat. Thankfully the class is focused on the presentation Tommy's giving on his pet armadillo. Ms. Graham asks Tommy a few follow-up questions about what kind of exercise armadillos like, and then she digs into the fishbowl of names she uses whenever she wants to call on us at random.

"Martina, you're our next presenter."

I stand and face my classmates. Most of them look expectantly in my direction, eager for a killer presentation from their class president.

There's just one problem.

My mind is blank.

I'm pretty sure the front row can hear my heart pounding inside my chest. I've got to buy some time!

"Whenever you're ready, Martina."

"Ms. Graham, I just remembered my mom dropped off my show-and-tell item in the office. Can I run and get it?"

Ms. Graham nods and her hand dives back into the fishbowl. "In the meantime we'll hear from . . ."

I don't hear which classmate is chosen to take my spot because I'm already running to my cubbie. I throw open the door and dig out my magical sheet of stickers. There's got to be something on there I can present.

I quickly scan the sheet. Not the ice cream; we've got a parking lot full of baked goods today. Calculator? Not exactly show-and-tell worthy. AHA! The ant farm! I can definitely talk about ants for five minutes.

I look both ways to make sure no one is coming down the hall.

whoosh! POOF! Bam!
The ANT FARM

comes to life in my hands. Thankfully it's normal size and not humongous and filled with gigantic ants like something out of a horror movie. (You can never tell with stickers.)

Hundreds of ants scurry through tunnels

behind the glass, bringing specks of sugar from a pyramid of sugar cubes at the top down to their nest at the bottom, like an assembly line.

I carefully walk the ant farm down the hall to my classroom, where Caitlyn is finishing her presentation on a luchador mask that was passed down from her great-grandmother.

"Take it away, Martina." Ms. Graham steps aside to give me the floor.

"The ants within this ant farm aren't just insects," I begin. "They're a team. They may be small on their own, but when they work together they can move mountains." I point to the pile of sugar cubes. "Or in this case, cubes of sugar."

"Those ants will make a great clean-up crew after the bake sale is over," Samantha says.

"The way the ants work together is exactly how everyone came together to make the bake sale a reality today," Ms. Graham adds.

Scott raises his hand. "So does that make you our queen, Martina?"

"No way," I answer. "This is a democracy!"

Ms. Graham asks me some follow-up questions about the habitat of ants. Lucky for me, I know enough basic facts to answer her.

Later, the afternoon bake sale turns out to be bigger than the one this morning. Even Noreen's quinoa date bars sell out, as well as the gluten-free sugar cookies and the vegan gingerbread.

As I'm giving José's dad his change, a woman in a fancy polka-dot top approaches the table holding up her phone.

"Which one of you made these videos?" she asks. Her hoop earrings dangle under her light-brown hair.

I pause for a moment before answering. Bev's eyes are wide and she looks almost terrified. *Did I do something wrong?*

I tell the woman I made the videos.

"These photos and videos are great. And smart for your school to be tagging me on social media."

The woman flips her sunglasses onto the top of her head like a headband. "We at *Cupcake*

82

Challenge would love to have a few contestants like you." She breaks into a smile and extends her hand.

"I thought it was you!" Bev jumps up and down and grabs the woman's arm before I can. "Martina, it's Christy Morales!"

With her sunglasses and yoga outfit I didn't recognize her, but sure enough it's the host of the web series *Cupcake Challenge*.

"You want US to be on your show?" I ask.

She puts a five-dollar bill on the table and picks up one of the Craig-inspired cupcakes. If she asks if I made them, should I say yes even though Nigel did the work?

I can feel Bev holding her breath, waiting for Christy's reaction.

"Your cupcakes are very good," Christy finally says. "But your social media campaign and video content are even better. We're starting a new series next week and still need a couple of whiz kids—what do you say?"

For all the things Bev and I have in common, we couldn't be more different in how we react when we're on the spot. Whenever I'm pushed anywhere near the center of attention, I shut down. It's like my personality runs and hides deep in the back of my mind until the spotlight passes and it's safe to come out again. Bev on the other hand can't stop talking to save her life. I can't believe the flood of information that pours out of her now.

"Martina and I love you!" Her arms flail wildly as she talks. "We watch every episode of your show as soon as it's uploaded! Well, except for last night's episode on desserts you can make in a mug because my mom made me help her organize her closet to take some stuff to Goodwill. But I eat desserts out of a mug all the time! I guess it's not exactly the same as actually making them in a mug, but Martina's the one with the culinary talent. Right, Martina?"

It takes me a while to recover from the avalanche of Bev's words and realize Christy is waiting for me to respond. "My parents own a diner," I finally answer.

"You two have great energy," Christy says. She crosses one arm over her waist and taps a finger on her bottom lip. "We've never had two contestants on the show who are friends."

"Friends?!" Bev wraps her arms around me in a death grip. "Martina and I are practically sisters!"

"So you're interested?" Christy lets out a small

laugh. "Great. Would it be okay if my team called your parents?"

We both shout a giant YES.

We're going to be contestants on our FAVOR-ITE web series!

CUPCAKE CHALLENGE,

getting Camera Ready

Even though we're both ready to make our official web series debut, Bev and I aren't allowed to be filmed without our parents' permission, so we e-mail the producers their contact info. Both my parents know how much I love watching people my age cook or bake online—ESPECIALLY on Christy Morales's show—so I know they'll let me compete. Since they'll make me promise my schoolwork won't suffer, I prepare a detailed calendar of when I'll be able to study. Dad's more excited than Mom and says yes before I even present my plan. I wonder if he hopes I'll follow him into the family business someday.

Bev's grades aren't as good as mine so her parents make her jump through a few more hoops—like fewer sleepovers and more conferences with Ms. Graham. But in the end, they say yes too. Bev comes over Saturday afternoon to share the good news, bringing the kittens along to play.

"We've got to figure out what to wear," she says. "And how we'll do our hair. I was thinking I'd wear mine down. Do you think they'll make us wear nets or hats so we don't get hair in the food?"

Bev's barely ever baked a potato—let alone a batch of Instagram-worthy cupcakes. I tell her job one is practicing our kitchen skills.

"Wrong," she says. "First and foremost, we need to look great."

"Are you thinking what I'm thinking?"

Bev nods. "Break out the stickers!"

I double-check that we're both thinking the same thing. "You're talking about the lipstick, right?"

Bev laughs. "No, let's cover ourselves in ice cream. OF COURSE the lipstick!"

Before I take out the sticker sheet, I look in on the kittens, who are quietly resting on my bed. They don't seem dangerous today and I hope they behave while Bev and I experiment with how we'll look on camera—as if my parents will ever let me wear makeup. But that doesn't stop me from peeling off the lipstick sticker anyway.

whoosh! POOF! Bam!

The tube of LIPSTICK

appears in my hand. It is a beautiful pink: not too bright, not too pale. The perfect color.

"You go first," Bev says.

I've never put on lipstick before so I need a mirror. The last thing I want is to be broadcast on computers and cell phones across the world with a pink, crooked smile like some clown. Bev and I go into the bathroom and take turns slowly putting color on our lips. Then we take Mom's hand mirror and go back to my room, admiring ourselves. We look great!

But something feels a little off. "I didn't think lipstick had a taste," I say.

"Sometimes it's cherry or vanilla flavored," Bev says, "but this is something else." She takes the tube from my hands, pops the cap back off, and sniffs. "It's definitely not cherry."

I run my tongue over my lips. "It kind of tastes like . . . tuna fish."

Before the word is out of my mouth, the two kittens pounce on us, licking our faces.

"Who would make tuna-fish lipstick?" Bev asks. "Worst. Idea. Ever!"

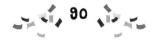

Burger and Fries are now in all-out lunch-time mode while Bev and I frantically fight them off. For kittens, they're amazingly strong and their tongues are scratchy and rough.

From the other end of the house, Lily hears the ruckus and comes racing into the room. My bed is suddenly a tornado of paws, whiskers, and tails.

When Bev and I get all three animals off us, we look at each other, stunned. With our disheveled hair, red faces, and smudged pink lipstick, we are anything but camera ready.

Eric sticks his head into my room on his way to work. He's been logging so many hours lately that I see him more in his coffee-shop clothes than his normal ones.

He looks at us and cringes. "Mom said you got on a cooking show—you sure it's not a horror series?"

"GO AWAY!" I scream. I'm too busy scrambling to hide the lipstick from the kittens to

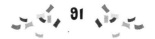

throw out a good comeback. I don't want the kittens to choke on the tube in their frenzy for more tuna fish.

I must've surprised Eric with how loud I yelled because he's speechless in the doorway, then walks off without a word.

I put the kittens in Lily's crate and poke my finger in to feel Burger's silky fur. "Why can't they be calm like this all the time?"

Nigel suddenly appears with a bucket and sponge. "I'm washing all the fingerprints off the light switches and doorknobs. Your room is next."

"WOW!" Bev springs up to greet my robot that used to be a sticker. "Pleasure to make your acquaintance, Nigel." She curtsies and speaks in a fake English accent.

Nigel's gumballs rumble in his head. "Are you mocking me?"

"No, I've just heard so much about you," Bev explains. "You make great cupcakes, by the way."

I tell Nigel that now isn't a good time to clean my room, but he gets to work anyway.

"It will take me 10.36 seconds to complete this task. There, all done. Tell your friend her accent was terrible."

Nigel zooms out of the room and down the hall.

Bev picks up the carrier as the kittens now gently snooze inside and says she's going home to finish her schoolwork. "I don't want to give my parents any reason to have second thoughts about *Cupcake Challenge*," she says.

That evening, Dad brings my abuelita over to watch the season finale of *Dancing with the Stars* and give us all haircuts. She's been trimming my brothers' and my hair since before I can remember. But now that Eric has his own money, he prefers to go to a real barber downtown.

I take a seat at our kitchen table and my grandmother drapes a towel over my chest. She struggles to brush my hair straight because it's filled with tangles from when I fought off the tuna-crazed kittens.

"Martina! What happened to your pretty hair?" She frowns and grabs a wider comb to work through the knots.

"Bev and I were playing with kittens," I say. "They kind of got out of control."

Dad comes in to grab a soda from the fridge. "Those kittens you had here the other day? I had a bad feeling about them."

Abuelita runs her hand down my arm to the beaded brace- let around my wrist. "You must be care- ful, Marti. Evil spir- its love a challenge."

I quickly change

the subject to the finale of *Dancing* and thankfully Abuelita doesn't mention evil spirits for the rest of the night.

But that doesn't mean I'm not still thinking about them. Am I asking for trouble by being on *Cupcake Challenge*?

I just hope the answer to this question doesn't reveal itself on camera.

The other contestants

Bev comes over on Saturday so we can hone our baking skills for the first competition. We spend the morning studying challenges from the last two seasons. If people across the country are going to watch us bake, we need to be ready for every holiday challenge, pastry puzzle, and surprise ingredient they throw at us.

"No ingredient is off-limits," I tell Bev. "We have to be ready to incorporate anything into a baked good."

The rest of the weekend is spent catching up

on homework and even reading ahead. I don't want to mess up my chance to appear on *Cupcake Challenge*.

Back in school on Monday, I promise myself not to say anything about getting chosen to be on the show until after the first episode airs, but Bev lets the cat out of the bag before reaching her desk.

"Guess what?" she shouts. "Martina and I are going to be on *Cupcake Challenge* and we start filming today!"

I get that Bev loves to be the center of attention; I just wish she didn't always have to drag me along with her.

"No way!" Samantha says. "Those kids make the cutest desserts!"

Ms. Graham is in shock. "Martina and Bev, this is incredible! When can we tune in?"

Bev answers for us. "What we film today should be uploaded to their channel next week. The producers shoot all three episodes before uploading any of them."

"This year has certainly been full of accomplishments," Ms. Graham says. "I was going to wait until this afternoon, but since we're already celebrating, Scott will tell us the final tally on the bake sale profits."

Scott rolls up a sheet of notebook paper into a makeshift megaphone and speaks into it. "As class treasurer, it is my pleasure to announce that our bake sale earned seven hundred and fifty-six dollars!"

The class explodes in cheers, and a huge smile spreads across my face. That number is a lot higher than I would have guessed!

"That means many more books for our school library," Ms. Graham says. "Great job, everyone."

98

I feel like I'm walking on clouds for the rest of the day, and that's BEFORE we go to *Cupcake Challenge*.

After school, Bev's mom drops us off at Christy Morales's studio, which is only a fifteen-minute drive from my house. Who knew the show I've been watching all this time is filmed so close by?

When the producers ask Bev and me if it's okay that we're on the same team, we both shout, "YES!" Actually it's MORE than okay—for me, it's absolutely necessary. I can't imagine being part of a real show without Bev taking the lead. If I'm lucky, I'll get to work in the background, prepping all the ingredients, while Bev's on camera doing all the talking.

The other two contestants are already in the studio when we get there. Sam is maybe a year older than we are and lives downtown in Little Tokyo. He's standing in front of a table full of colorful squares that he's making into tiny origami sculptures.

"I put these on all my cupcakes," he says.

"You should see what he can do with cupcake liners," the cameraperson says. "He just made the most beautiful swan I've ever seen!"

In the thirty seconds it takes for us to introduce ourselves, Sam's hands move quietly and swiftly to make a gorgeous hummingbird. If his baking is as good as his origami, Bev and I are in trouble.

Next to him is a girl wearing thick black glasses and a lab coat. Her hair is tied back. "I'm Simone," she says. "Sam and I go to the same school, but we don't really know each other."

As we talk, she unpacks a large Styrofoam cooler with the kind of glass beakers and containers you see in a laboratory.

"Are you sure you're here for *Cupcake Challenge*?" Bev asks. "Looks more like *Bill Nye the Science Guy*."

Simone doesn't crack a smile. She just sets out a Bunsen burner and some tongs.

"My mom won't even let me hold a match, never mind light one," I whisper to Bev. "I hope

100

Simone doesn't blow us all up." I suddenly won-der if Bev and I are prepared for the level of com-petition in this online show.

Christy breezes into the room so relaxed, you'd never know she was about to go on cam-era. She introduces the four of us to the director and producer, as well as the rest of the crew. Sam and Simone are involved in their projects and barely look up.

"Each episode will revolve around a different theme," Christy begins. "But I won't tell you what it is until the cameras are rolling."

I close my eyes and hope today's theme doesn't involve origami or science. On *Cupcake Wars*, a baking show on TV, contestants have to make 1,000 cupcakes in the final round. We're not going to have to do anything like that, are we?

Christy shows us around the set, which consists of two identical kitchens. Bev and I can't contain our excitement. We're actually standing in the kitchens we've watched on YouTube hundreds of times!

"All the ingredients are here to make any kind of cupcake you could possibly imagine." Christy points to a giant digital clock on the wall and tells us we'll need to monitor our time as we go. "For the first round, you'll have forty-five minutes."

"That's not enough time to bake a quality

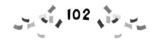

cupcake," Craig whispers from my bag. "You can't rush these things!"

I knew taking Craig along today was risky, but he insisted, saying he'd be able to give me an inside track. "You have a talking cupcake as a resource and you're not going to use him?" he asked. Bev wholeheartedly agreed, so along he came.

lights.
camera.
action!

The secret Ingredient

"We're going to take it easy on you kids since today's the first day," Christy says. "The most important thing is to have fun."

Between our super-smart competitors and all the cameras and lights, having fun seems less important than just surviving.

"You've watched the show so you know the format," Christy continues. "Each team will be judged on creativity and taste." She talks to the director and asks if he's ready. I secretly hope he's not because I suddenly feel hot, nervous, and about to pass out.

But the director IS ready, so Christy moves to the center of the kitchen.

"Hello! And welcome to another episode of *Cupcake Challenge*," Christy says into the camera. "We've got some new contestants for the next three episodes competing for a secret grand prize worth up to five thousand dollars!"

I was so excited just to be on the show that I totally forgot about the prize! Kids on the show in the past have won scholarships and cupcake parties for their whole school. I try not to focus on the prize but on the task at hand.

"Before we get baking," Christy announces, "let's meet our competitors."

I've watched this show enough to know that the contestants have to introduce themselves in the first episode—not to mention keep a running commentary on the cupcake creations. If I get through this part, I hope Bev can do the rest.

Neither Simone nor Sam seems nervous as they casually tell our future viewers where they're from, what school they go to, and what else they do besides cook. Simone is super focused, whereas Sam calmly rolls a sheet of black-and-white paper into a beautiful zebra.

Then Christy smiles and turns toward me. My hands feel clammy and I know the director will have to yell "CUT" because I'll still be standing there like a scarecrow with nothing to say.

I hear a voice say, "I've got this." At first I think it's Bev, but it's Craig, who can throw his voice like an expert ventriloquist.

"My name is Martina Rivera," Craig says in a perfect imitation of me. "And my favorite thing in the world is cupcakes!" I have no idea what Craig's going to say for me, so I lip-sync a few beats behind him.

"CUT!" The director pulls his headphones off and calls to a man with the most pockets on a pair of shorts I've ever seen. "Hey, Andy, the sound is off."

While the crew works, I excuse myself and hurry to the restroom to pull Craig out of my bag.

"I know you're trying to help but stop talking for me!" I scold. "You're making it worse."

Who would've thought a cupcake would ruin everything ON A SHOW ABOUT CUPCAKES? Craig tries to jump out of my bag but I don't let him.

"You'd better suit up for the game, Martina," Craig says. "You're NOT going to make me look bad on YouTube!"

"You're not even on the show!" I immediately lower my voice when the restroom door opens. Luckily it's Bev, checking on me.

"Come on, Martina, you can do this," she says. "Let's get these introductions over with."

"That means Little Miss Introvert has to bring her A game," Craig says.

"What's with all the sports metaphors?" I ask.

Craig looks at me sheepishly. "I've been watching a lot of basketball."

I roll my eyes and zip my bag.

Bev looks concerned and asks if I'm okay. I tell her I'm as good as I'm going to get. Then I head back to the set.

When the director calls action, this time I'm the one introducing myself, not Craig. I nervously rush through it and then the camera shifts to Bev. She's in her element and makes the crew laugh during her intro so she has to tape again.

Christy takes a *Cupcake Challenge* gift box off one of the kitchen shelves and sets it on the counter. "Is everybody ready for the first task?"

All four of us nod. Christy pulls the ribbon off the gift box.

"The theme for today is . . . cauliflower!"

She yanks on the ribbon and the front of the box falls open to reveal a big, lumpy head of cauliflower. From inside my bag I hear Craig yell, "That's just wrong!"

I couldn't agree more.

"GO!"

Christy hits the giant timer on the wall and our forty-five minutes begin. Nigel may have baked the cupcakes that got me onto the show, but I'm on my own now.

Bev looks at me for a plan but the clock is ticking so I race to the cupboards and grab some ingredients instead. I've never had such a short deadline to bake. Not to mention the worst theme for cupcakes EVER. Why couldn't we get cereal or gummy bears like the last show?

"Cauliflower is disgusting," Bev says. "What are we going to do?"

I actually like cauliflower but now isn't the time to argue because I'm too busy whisking eggs and oil.

"We can steam the cauliflower and shred it into the batter," I tell Bev.

"What's going on out there?" Craig yells from inside my bag. "What happened to good old-fashioned chocolate?"

"Cauliflower doesn't have a strong taste after

it's cooked," I say. "Chocolate will cover it up but we'll still be including it in the recipe."

Bev doesn't look convinced. "I don't know . . . How about we throw in some extra chocolate chips, just to be sure?"

We steam the cauliflower. Then I measure and mix ingredients in a large bowl while Bev preheats the oven and grabs our muffin tins, which are already filled with cupcake liners bearing the show's logo. Bev spoons our cauliflower cake batter into the cups and I peek into my bag to check on Craig to see if he has any last-minute tips.

"Never overbake a cupcake," he says. "You'll end up with a lump of charcoal."

I look over at Simone and Sam, who are working seamlessly with precision and speed. They've barely said a word to each other since the clock started.

"It looks like they're using mustard." Bev squints to see their station better. "What have they got up their sleeves?"

With our tins in the oven, I wipe the flour and eggshells off the countertop. Christy comes over and turns on the oven light to check our progress.

"Sprinkles!" She clasps her hands together. "What a great idea to put chocolate sprinkles with cauliflower."

Bev waits for Christy to move to the other team's oven before asking me what Christy's talking about. "We didn't use sprinkles," Bev says.

I open the oven door and pull out the rack with our cupcakes. Sure enough, every cupcake is covered in sprinkles.

Lots of sprinkles.

Sprinkles that are MOVING.

NO NO NO! I race to my bag, which is slung over the corner of the baking table. The ant farm I used for show-and-tell is sticking out, and several rows of ants are marching across the stainless-steel surface into the bowl of batter.

Bev suddenly looks nauseous. "I licked the

 111

spoon and bowl after I poured the batter," she says. "Do you think I swallowed any ants?!"

This is a disaster!

When we take the trays out of the oven, the cupcakes look surprisingly good. The ants are now swirled through the batter in bursts of geometric shapes. They don't even look like ants anymore, just sprinkles.

"Are we going to tell Christy?" Bev asks. "Or let her eat a mouthful of insects?"

I have no idea what we should do. Across the room, Simone and Sam are explaining their creations to Christy. Bev and I only have a minute to figure out a plan.

"The origami on the top is obviously in the shape of a cauliflower," Sam says. "I used a deep yellow paper because cauliflower is in the mustard family."

We're going to get beat. Why did I think this was a good idea?

"We used a laser tape measure to make sure the peaks in our frosting were evenly constructed," Simone says. "Each cupcake is topped with vanilla buttercream in the shape of a cauliflower floret."

As Christy comes to our side of the kitchen, I can almost see the wheels spinning inside Bev's head.

"Interesting," Christy says when she sees our final product. "What can you tell us about your ingredients?"

"We used cauliflower and chocolate to make our cupcakes." Bev lifts one of them off the platter and offers it to our host.

"This looks delicious," Christy says.

"Very healthy too," Bev continues. "Lots of *ant*ibodies to keep your immune system up."

I cringe at Bev's joke. Are we going to let Christy actually eat the insect sprinkles?!

"You have to stop her!" Craig screams from my bag. "You're giving cupcakes a bad name!"

Christy takes a giant bite and almost swoons. "The chocolate sprinkles add a nice crunch to the smooth cauliflower." She puts the rest of the cupcake back on the platter. "Our first competition is certainly a difficult one to judge," Christy says into the camera.

"Not really," Bev whispers.

"But I'm going to give today's round to Simone and Sam for their beautiful presentation and tasty

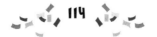

creation. Tune in next week to see what we cook up on a new episode of *Cupcake Challenge*!" Christy turns to Bev and me. "But great job, girls. This round was a tough call."

"That's a wrap," the director says as a clean-up crew comes in to wipe down the kitchen.

Bev looks as shocked as I am that Christy hasn't gotten sick. "Do you think they really did turn into sprinkles when we baked them?" Bev asks.

As nervous as I am to find out for sure, I know there's only one way to tell. I pick up a cupcake from our plate and look at it closely. It takes everything I've got to work up the courage to bring it to my lips and take a small bite.

"Well?" Bev asks.

I take another bite. If there ARE ants in this, no one would ever be able to tell. They taste like roasted chocolate.

Bev and I race down to the parking lot before anything else happens with my magical—and troublesome—stickers.

"That was a close call," Bev says. "We can't afford any more mistakes."

"It's a crime!" Craig shouts. "You should both be in dessert prison!"

But all I'm thinking about is how I just served my show-and-tell ant farm on our cooking show.

Dad's
New BFF

When Dad picks us up, he's eager to hear how the first episode of *Cupcake Challenge* went. I tell him I don't want to talk about it; Bev is surprisingly quiet too. After today's disaster, all I want to do is hide under the covers in my room, but Dad tells me that once we drop off Bev, we have to pick up Eric and Nigel at the diner.

"It seems like you've had Nigel quite a while," Dad says as we drive. "Don't the other kids want to take him home too?"

I tell Dad my classmates would love to spend

time with Nigel—which would probably be true if any of them knew he existed. "I'll have to give him up soon," I say—which is ALSO true if the rules of my other sticker sheets apply.

When we get to the diner, I'm surprised to see a large, shiny cappuccino machine behind the counter. Eric works the knobs with a focus I've never seen him have before. He hands my father a small latte.

"Check that out, Marti!" Dad tilts his cup toward me and I'm shocked to see a perfectly shaped rose in the foam on top of the coffee.

"You're a coffee artist!" I tell Eric. "I had no idea you were so good."

Dad agrees and sips the coffee. His eyes close as he savors the taste. "Wonderful, *mijo*," he tells Eric. "Being able to offer different kinds of coffee to our customers might help bring in business."

I stare at the fancy contraption now taking up half the counter and ask Dad how he could afford such an expensive new machine. Before

he can answer, Nigel comes out from the back room wearing a welding mask.

"Nigel built it." Dad smiles. "Is there anything this guy CAN'T do?"

Nigel technically isn't a "guy" but I have to agree: he's by far the most talented sticker I've ever had. (Sorry, Craig.)

"We mostly do flowers and birds in the foam at work," Eric says. "But Nigel tells me there's no limit to the designs I can do in the milk."

"A coffee master too!" Dad puts his arm around Nigel, his new best friend. "Where have you been all our lives, Nigel?"

Lately my biggest worry has been Dad's finances. But now I'm more concerned he's going to be heartbroken when Nigel suddenly disappears.

On the drive home, Dad starts singing, which he only does when he's really happy. At the chorus, Nigel harmonizes along in perfect Spanish.

As we whiz by the rows of palm trees outside the car, I try to figure out how I can take advantage of Nigel on *Cupcake Challenge*. Is it too late to sign up an additional member of our baking team? Should Bev and I be practicing our skills with him every night? Should I be calling him from the studio to find out what to do with crazy ingredients like cauliflower?

When they stop singing, Nigel announces that as much as he loves helping out at the diner, he's got to get to work on the robotics lab at our school.

"This week?" Dad asks.

"That's correct, William," Nigel answers. "My work awaits."

I'm torn. I don't want Dad relying on Nigel too much—especially since they're apparently on a first-name basis—but I'm also afraid if we don't keep Nigel busy, he'll start bossing around the kids at school and make them build him a robotics lab. I tell Nigel it's okay with me if he wants to work at the diner instead.

He turns to face me in the backseat with his metallic eyes. "I've got MY work to do too," Nigel says. "You want me to achieve MY goals, don't you?"

Dad answers for me. "Of course we do! Let us know how we can help, buddy. Right, Martina?"

If Nigel had eyebrows, they'd be arched as he waits for my answer.

"The robotics lab it is," I say.

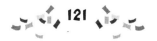

Nigel turns back around in his seat and starts singing along with a new song on the radio that Dad joins in on.

How am I going to explain a pushy robot to my teachers?

An Old Family Recipe

The next episode of *Cupcake Challenge* doesn't take place on the usual set. Instead it's filmed in the kitchen of Christy's Bakery in Beverly Hills. Bev's never been to the bakery before and is shocked by the long line of locals and tourists outside.

As we walk through the bustling kitchen, I'm surprised to see Debbie, who used to waitress at the diner. She puts down the giant tray of cupcakes she's holding and gives me a big hug.

Debbie starts jumping up and down when she hears I'm one of the new contestants.

"You've always had great baking skills," she says. "I can't wait until Christy posts your episodes."

It's nice to see Debbie surrounded by so much activity. I introduce her to Bev, who's setting up our side of the kitchen for today's challenge.

Sam and Simone are ahead of us in the competition and they're determined to win this afternoon too. They both wheel in giant suitcases, which they proceed to empty onto the counter: pastry bags with hundreds of decorative tips, marzipan, frosting spatulas, and more jars of candy than the drugstore sells at Halloween. All Bev and I have are our schoolbags and Craig.

"You know, I'm not a fan, but this is one instance where Nigel might be helpful," Craig complains. "I don't know how to make myself more clear: I cannot be part of a team that loses on a show called *Cupcake Challenge*!"

I zip my bag closed; the last thing I need is more pressure right now.

Christy waits for the signal from the director, then talks into the camera. "We really threw our contestants a curveball with cauliflower last week," she begins. "We're going back to basics for this episode and filming right here in the kitchen of our world famous bakery. Our viewers who have visited Christy's Bakery in person may have noticed our one-of-a-kind cupcake ATM out front—that stands for automated treat machine." Christy winks. "The winner of today's competition will get an ever-sweeter victory because their tasty creation will be featured in our cupcake ATM for a whole week!"

A chance to get our cupcakes in the ATM? This is incredible!

I hear Bev gasp. Sam and Simone fist-bump. I'm just glad our cauliflower-and-ant cupcakes won't be in the running this time.

Christy reaches into the cabinet and hands both teams a large bundle of cinnamon sticks.

"Cinnamon has been used for centuries," she says. "Today we'll see your modern take on it."

Before Bev and I can huddle to come up with a plan, Sam and Simone have put their cinnamon sticks in some kind of vapor chamber, probably trying to reduce the flavor to its essence.

"How about sugar and cinnamon?" Bev asks. "Those are my favorite kind of Pop-Tarts."

"No one cares about Pop-Tarts right now," Craig yells from inside my bag.

I can't think of cinnamon without thinking of my favorite food in the world: churros. I can almost taste the fried dough covered with cinnamon and sugar that my abuelita makes whenever I sleep over. Some people might be lured from their beds by the aroma of bacon or coffee, but for me it's churros.

"Why don't we bake our cupcakes with churro batter?" I suggest to Bev. "I'll start the mixture while you grate the cinnamon."

Bev isn't too happy when I escort her away from the food processor to the hand grater. She waves her fingers in the air and tells me she and her mom just went for manicures.

"Sorry, Bev. We're going old-school today."

I smile as I measure the flour, knowing my abuelita would be proud. Bev has such a hard time with the grater that she ends up using the spice grinder, which works almost as well.

"I love the idea of churro cupcakes," Bev says. "But we're going to need more than that." She points to Simone, who's taking out a small kitchen blowtorch, sending the producers racing across the set with a fire extinguisher. "I know the ant farm was a mistake," Bev continues, "but is there anything else on that sheet that can help us?"

Of course!

We can bake the churro cupcakes, scoop out some of the inside, and fill each one with a dollop of ice cream.

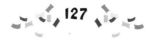

Craig yells at me for disrupting his view as I grab the magical sheet of stickers from my bag.

whoosh! POOF! BAM!

Instantly I'm holding a perfectly shaped vanilla

"Do you think this is cheating?" I ask Bev.

"No way! Look at all the stuff Simone and Sam brought in!"

As she examines the cone in my hands, I know what she's thinking: *Will the ice cream never run out, like the pizza and lemonade stickers on my other magic sheets?*

There's only one way to find out.

As soon as we pull the churro cupcakes from the oven, Bev and I grab a couple of knives and start cutting the tops off each cupcake. I look over at the clock and realize we have only four minutes left.

"Make sure to save the tops," I yell to Bev. "We'll need to cover up the holes once we fill them with ice cream."

Bev and I work so fast, we spill several scoops on the floor. Lucky for us, the magic ice cream cone doesn't run out.

We replace the tops of the churro cupcakes, then frost them with the cinnamon frosting

we made while the cupcakes were in the oven. There's no time to spare—which is good because Christy needs to taste them before the ice cream melts.

The buzzer goes off and several of Christy's staff applaud. When I spot Debbie in the doorway, she gives me a thumbs-up.

"Let's start with last episode's winners," Christy says. "And what is THAT?!" Bev and I have been so busy filling our cupcakes with ice cream that we missed what Sam and Simone have created on the other side of the room.

"Is that a mummy?" Bev asks.

Sure enough, the other team has created a giant cupcake in the shape of a mummy. For a minute I wonder if that's within the rules, but then remember we're using ice cream that was previously a sticker.

"Cinnamon was first used in ancient Egypt in 2000 BC," Simone begins. "They ate it, wore it, and even embalmed people with it."

Bev leans over and whispers in my ear. "You sure you don't want to switch teams? You and Simone are like two nerds in a pod."

I'm embarrassed to admit I DID know that fact about ancient Egyptians. But never in a million years would I have thought about using cinnamon bark to wrap a mummy cupcake.

"Top marks for presentation," Christy says. "Let's see how it tastes."

Bev and I hold our breath as Christy takes a bite.

"Good," she says. "But the cinnamon could've been ground a bit finer. It's a little bitter."

Simone looks like she wants to wrap herself in cinnamon bark and jump on the table alongside the mummy.

Sam's expression is more *I-told-you-so*.

"Now let's check out Bev and Martina." Christy holds up one of our cupcakes and takes a tiny taste. "Is this churro batter? Very innovative—and a perfect use for cinnamon." She takes a small bite, not enough to taste the ice cream filling.

I nudge Bev to tell Christy to take another bite but she just shakes her head as if to say telling Christy is MY job.

"There's a surprise inside each cupcake," I finally say.

Christy takes another bite. "Vanilla ice cream! And it's the perfect consistency—not too frozen, not too melted.

"Another tough choice," Christy continues. "But the winners of this round are Martina and Bev—and the people of Los Angeles, who can buy one of their churro cupcakes in our Christy's Bakery ATM all week! Even if we have to leave out the ice cream, this cupcake is a winner."

Bev and I hug and scream. From the sidelines, Debbie hoots and hollers. There's never an audience at the tapings so it's nice to have some in-person support.

"The next episode will be our final challenge for these contestants," Christy says into the camera. "And with each team scoring one victory, the title of cupcake champ could go to either one of them." She pulls Bev, Sam, Simone, and me into a group hug.

"The next challenge will test more than just your baking. It involves social media, pictures, and an art installation. We'll be inviting the public too. Are the contestants ready?"

We all smile and shout, "Yes!" but inside, one word ricochets through my body.

NOOOOOOO!

Helping Hands

The next day, Mom, Dad, and I meet Bev and her parents outside Christy's store for the unveiling of our churro cupcakes in the automated treat machine. Christy's producer films on her phone and tells us the video will be featured as a bonus segment online when the episodes are uploaded.

We take a zillion photos in front of the machine with Bev and me pointing to our winning cupcake. Bev's dad is so proud, he buys half a dozen from the machine before Christy tells him we're welcome to take home as many as we'd like for the rest of the family. It's exciting, but I wish my abuelita wasn't traveling to Mexico City with two girlfriends and could be here to celebrate. After all, we really owe this victory to her delicious churro recipe.

As we head back to our car, I twirl the bracelet around my wrist. I haven't taken it off since it came to life. Maybe Abuelita is right and it IS bringing me good luck.

On Monday, Bev is waiting at my cubbie with a carved wooden totem pole the size of a ruler. The faces are all cats, so it's pretty obvious whose handiwork this is.

"You've got to be kidding," I tell Bev. "I don't know whether to be impressed or terrified."

"I'm worried they'll find my dad's power tools," Bev says.

I suddenly spot Nigel wheeling a shopping cart full of motherboards and circuits into Mr. Lynch's old room in the back of the building.

Principal Lajoie follows closely behind. "Why didn't I hear about this robotics lab?"

"You might want to call the superintendent." Nigel flashes the lanyard he's wearing around his neck. "But I think your approval rating is so high, the committee decided this school would be a great site to test the program."

Principal Lajoie smiles, then heads back to her office to follow up.

I race down the hall after Nigel. "How'd you get an official pass? You have to stop before you get in trouble!"

Nigel smirks. "Don't you mean before YOU get in trouble?"

As soon as he unpacks an electronic gizmo from the cart, I swipe it out of his hands. Nigel looks at me with exasperation. "We're already a big hit. Come look."

He leads me to the cafeteria, where two new identical robots with gumball-machine heads are helping the lunch ladies set up. Mrs. Cordeiro is laughing at something one of the robots said; the

whole group seems to be productive and having fun.

"And how about this?" Nigel leads me to the front office, where another robot is sorting mail while Ms. Harrison files alongside him.

"How did you build new robots so fast?" I ask him. "It's your first day here!"

Nigel gives me a sly smile. "You just need the right tools. Get used to seeing us around—there'll be even more of us by this afternoon."

I'm glad the new robots are helping out these hardworking staffers, but I feel anxious knowing that all this additional—and free—help will most likely disappear soon. There's something underneath that feeling too; I can't put my finger on it, but I don't like the way Nigel's android efficiency has gone from cooperative to sneaky within a week's time.

Most of our morning class is spent talking about the robots. Do we get to take them home? Can they help with our homework? Can they sub when a teacher is sick? Bewildered, Ms. Graham

has no answers and steers the conversation toward choosing new books for our school library.

She makes a list on the smartboard of our suggestions—everything from picture books to graphic novels to a new chapter-book series about baby animals. I suggest one or two titles but mostly listen to my classmates. It makes me proud to think all these new books are a direct result of our bake sale.

During our free time, Ms. Santos lets us do our math homework. I've been spending so much time working on *Cupcake Challenge* that I feel behind in my schoolwork. I usually don't have a hard time with multiplication tables but for some reason the seven table completely escapes me. After 7×3, I struggle with the rest of the table, erasing my initial guesses so many times that I tear the worksheet. Why is math so difficult today?

Hey, wait a minute . . . one of my last three magical stickers is a calculator!

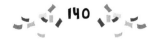

Ms. Santos isn't a big fan of us using calculators in class, but she also knows that some kids really need them. So much of my brain has been taken up with cupcakes lately that I'll take all the help I can get.

I rummage through my bag and pull out the magic sheet.

The only stickers left are the wave and the baseball bat. WHAT HAPPENED TO THE CALCULATOR? Did I forget I peeled it off? I'll have to try my best on the sevens table and ask Craig as soon as I get home.

But I don't have to wait that long. On my way out of class, I spot Nigel near my cubby, accompanied by four new robots.

"How are you making these robots so fast?" I ask again.

"I'm just that good," he answers.

His posture seems strange, his hands crossed behind his back. When I ask if he's hiding something, he immediately denies it.

I pretend to leave, then spin around behind him. "You took my calculator!"

He holds the calculator over my head, out of reach. "It's just as much mine as yours," Nigel says. "We're from the same sheet! Besides, it was sticking out of your bag!"

I've always wondered if the stickers could come alive without me and they obviously can. When Nigel peeled it off, did the calculator make the same

whoosh! poof! Bam!

the other stickers made?

My mind moves from the sticker process to the calculator. If there was a bulb hovering above my head, it would be lighting up now. "You're using this calculator to multiply these robots—you're not building them at all!"

I jump to reach the calculator but Nigel opens the top of his head and drops the calculator inside with the colorful gumballs. "I'm multiplying

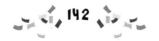

these robots to help your school!" Nigel says. "Two of them just shelved all the books in the library while another one repaired the play structure outside. With all the budget cuts this school has had, you should be thanking me, not complaining!"

Maybe Nigel's onto something—maybe I should take advantage of him while he's here. And since I'm student council president, the more things he does for our school the better, I guess.

Am I crazy to trust a robot?

money problems

As the week goes by, I feel like I might've jumped to conclusions about Nigel. The entire school buzzes with the energy of tasks getting done and repairs being made by his band of helpful androids. Rumor has it that one of the robots even graded Mr. Morelli's fifth-grade history test. Even though he lied about peeling off one of my stickers, Nigel has almost become part of the family. Last night he even took a break and watched *Dancing with the Stars* with Mom and me, shouting at the television when our favorite couple got eliminated.

There are supposed to be only three episodes in *Cupcake Challenge*, but the producer asks us to come into the bakery before our last showdown to tape a special segment where Christy gives us our assignments for the finale. Bev and I have watched enough episodes to know how complicated the last show can be. Rather than a secret ingredient, the final challenge always involves an elaborate theme. Last season's topic was Broadway and the two teams made cupcakes on subjects as varied as *SpongeBob* and *Hamilton*. Bev and I have been practicing our speed in the kitchen and we've definitely gotten better—I'm just not sure our abilities are good enough for us to beat Sam and Simone.

The producer tells us Christy has two meetings before ours and to sit tight. Sam takes out a stack of papers and starts folding to pass the time; Simone puts on headphones and listens to music. Bev makes small talk with Toni, the cameraperson, while Toni checks her frame and adjusts where we'll stand. I smile and pretend to listen to them chitchat about their favorite desserts but my mind is racing with guesses of what the theme will be.

"Sorry, kids," Christy says as she clatters in on high heels. "Franchises, pop-ups, online sales—the to-do list never ends!" She applies lipstick from her purse and it makes me wish the only lipstick I own didn't reek of tuna fish.

Christy stands in front of the velvet curtain and waits until Toni gives her the signal. She flashes her winning smile. "Is everyone excited to hear about the last challenge?"

It's not that I'm afraid of losing; I'm worried my stickers might cause some major disaster during the show. Bev, on the other hand, just seems happy to be here. It must be amazing to go through life without worrying all the time.

"The topic for the final challenge is . . . Los Angeles!" Christy reaches behind her and pulls

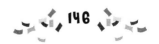

the curtain back, exposing a map of the city. "You've got a lot to choose from," she continues. "The Hollywood Walk of Fame, Santa Monica Pier, Malibu, the Hollywood sign, the mountains, Disneyland—the inspiration is endless."

Sam and Simone are typing furiously, while Bev does a little dance to show how excited she is. I smile and pretend to dance along but most of what I feel is dread.

"There's one more surprise," Christy says. "Each team gets to invite an additional person to help them complete the challenge. Friend, family, neighbor—as long as he or she isn't a professional pastry chef!"

Of course the first person I think of is Dad; he's not a pastry chef but he's the best cook I know. Whomever Sam and Simone get to help them will never match Dad in the kitchen. When Bev winks at me from across the counter, I know she's thinking the same thing.

On the drive home, Dad almost has to pull over when I tell him the final challenge will be filmed next Friday.

"That's the only day I CAN'T do," Dad says. "I have a big meeting at the bank to renegotiate the terms of my loan. I already had to change the meeting once—I can't do it again."

He seems as upset as I am.

"You have to!" I cry. "You're the only one who can help us win!"

Dad promises to call the bank and see if

they have any flexibility. "If they don't extend my loan, I'll lose the diner. It's an important meeting."

I turn to Bev, who's surprisingly silent. Who will help us if my dad can't?

My abuelita!

But from the backseat, Bev moves her arms stiffly; I'm about to tell her to stop being so weird when I realize she's acting like a robot. Who would be better in the challenge—my grandmother or Nigel?

While Dad calls the bank, Bev and I race through the house looking for Nigel. The door to my room is closed—is he in there?

It takes both Bev and me to push open the bedroom door. At first I think it's because the door is catching on the carpet, but when we finally squeeze inside we discover the room is jam-packed with robots. In the center of the room is Nigel, furiously typing into the magic calculator that used to be a sticker.

"WHAT ARE YOU DOING?" I ask.

"There wasn't enough room at the robotics lab so we had to come here," Nigel answers. "I'm almost done. We'll be out of your way soon."

Bev drags me over to a corner of the room where two robots that look exactly like Nigel are alphabetizing the books on my shelf. "If your dad can't do the show with us, I'm sure one of these robots can."

I cross the room and grab the calculator from Nigel; I appreciate how many things he's helped with around the house and the diner but he's not the one in charge of these stickers—I am.

Dad hurries down the hall, putting an end to my staredown with Nigel. I leave Bev with Nigel and follow Dad.

"I'm sorry, Marti," he says. "If I want to keep the diner, I can't change the meeting."

I've been so focused on cupcakes and stickers that I've overlooked the fact that Dad might lose the business he's worked so hard for. I tell him it's okay, that we'll find someone else.

"How about Abuelita?" I ask.

Dad tells me my grandmother and her friends were having so much fun, they extended their stay in Mexico City.

Worst. News. Ever.

A little later, Eric knocks on my door. "Dad told me you need help on your cupcake show," he says. "I'm in."

Did I just hear that right? My big brother actually wants to help me?

"Don't look so surprised," Eric says. "You're not the only one who inherited Dad's culinary talents."

Dad comes into my room and puts an arm around each of us.

"My two big kids, working together. I'm so proud!"

I ask Eric why he suddenly insists on helping me.

"I've helped you do a ton of stuff," he answers. "Ride a bike, for one thing."

"Actually, that was me," Dad says. "But you definitely ran alongside Martina, encouraging her."

I can see Bev is also wondering why my brother who usually torments me is volunteering his time in our hour of need.

Eric laughs. "Between the diner and the coffee shop, my cooking skills have gotten pretty good. I'll be able to help you."

Dad agrees, telling us that Eric's lattes and cappuccinos have definitely brought new customers into the diner. "Besides, what goes better with a cupcake than a great cup of coffee?"

"Milk?" Bev and I respond.

"AND coffee," Eric adds. He smiles and for a minute I glimpse the old baseball-card-collecting brother who used to lift me up to reach the cereal cabinet, not the one who just hides behind a closed door texting his friends.

I turn to Bev, who shrugs and says okay.

After Eric leaves, Bev asks what kind of LA theme we should do.

Thinking about Eric's childhood obsession with baseball cards gives me an idea. I have two stickers left and the final challenge might be

the place to use one of them. "How about the Dodgers?" I ask. "We can do a whole baseball theme."

Bev jumps at the idea. She and her family have season tickets and go to every game. As she runs through suggestions, I dig out the sheet of magical stickers. Before I peel off the baseball bat, I close my eyes and hope it can help us win on *Cupcake Challenge*.

The

baseball bat

appears in my
hands looking like
every other baseball
bat I've ever seen.

"Should we try it out?"
Bev asks. "After all this thinking, I'd love some exercise."

We go to the backyard with the

kittens and I grab some of Eric's softballs from the garage. When he was younger, he used to play all the time. Bev pitches me one of the balls and I hit it across the yard on my first try. I'm not sure I've even played softball before. This MUST be a magic bat.

Eric and James spot us from the kitchen window and join in. I still have no idea how the bat will help in our challenge but at least we're having fun. Eric picks up a ball and gently tosses it toward me. I swing and send it flying into the neighbor's yard.

Eric grins from ear to ear. "I had no idea you were so good, Martina!"

I say thank you but I know my miraculous abilities are all thanks to the magic bat that used to be a sticker.

"Hey, Martina—don't forget to put the cupcakes away," Dad calls from the house.

James runs inside and emerges with a plastic plate of treats.

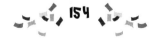

"Smash cupcakes!" he says.

Bev immediately knows what he's asking for, and as soon as James picks up the bat she pitches him a cupcake.

SMASH! James nails the cupcake on the first swing and shrieks with laughter when it explodes in front of him. I laugh too, but inside I'm thankful Craig isn't around to see this.

"That's what we should do for the finale," Bev says. "Have a cupcake batting cage!"

I'm already way ahead of her. If we use the calculator sticker, we can make hundreds of cupcakes for the visitors and judges to smash. Kids would love batting practice with cupcakes—especially if there are still enough left to eat.

Before I can share my idea, I notice the kittens across the yard in the sandbox. My mouth hangs open as I look at their latest construction project.

"That's . . . Dodger Stadium," Bev says.

Sure enough, the kittens have sculpted an exact replica, including the stadium's wavy rooftops.

"How did they know we were talking about baseball?" Bev asks.

"Too bad we can't take it out of the sandbox," I say. "It would make a great centerpiece for the final challenge."

"Maybe they can make one out of cupcake batter." Bev throws another cupcake to James, who's begging for the next pitch.

I run through all the ingredients we've discussed and come up with something that will dazzle the judges.

"How about Dodger Stadium made out of cotton candy?" I ask. "Between that and the cupcake batting cage, we'll have the most spectacular exhibit ever."

I sit down next to James, who's on the grass stuffing chunks of splattered cupcakes into his mouth. I reach over and eat one too. "Fun AND delicious," I say. "Let's get started."

Batter Up!

There's no way that during the finale we can bake enough cupcakes to fill a batting cage, so Bev and I spend the next few afternoons baking stockpiles of cupcakes with the ingredients provided by Christy's Bakery.

"I guess it's not a big deal if they're a little stale," Bev says as we stack a few boxes of cupcakes on the table. "It's not like the baseball bat can taste them."

After I ask Dad if we can borrow the diner's

old cotton candy machine, Bev and I spin several bags of cotton candy for Burger and Fries to sculpt. We use a giant tray from the diner as the base and the kittens do another perfect replica of Dodger Stadium in less than two hours. Bev and I add some edible glitter for a Dodger-blue finishing touch. Sam and Simone are going to have a tough time topping this.

With one day left before the finale, we start decorating our batches of chocolate cupcakes with vanilla frosting. Then we garnish the tops with red licorice laces arranged to look like stitches on a baseball. By the time we're finished, the cupcakes look perfect.

Eric borrows the catering van from the coffee shop to transport the cupcakes, the cotton candy sculpture, and the rest of our baking supplies to the studio. This final episode isn't being filmed in the same kitchen where we had our previous challenges, but on a large soundstage where networks often film game shows.

When we get there, Bev and I are shocked at how huge the space is.

"And I thought the bakery kitchen was big," Bev says.

The giant room is divided in half; Sam and Simone are already setting up their side.

"We're early and they STILL got here first," Bev whispers. "I hope we don't get creamed today."

"Another cupcake joke." Craig pops out from one of the trays. Since yesterday, Craig's new game is to hide among the hundreds of other cupcakes, then jump out to surprise us.

"You better stay down," I tell him, "or you might end up getting used for batting practice."

Craig immediately jumps into the nearest box as Nigel appears with a clipboard and headset. "We're beginning in twenty minutes. Will you girls be ready?"

"WHAT ARE YOU DOING HERE?" I ask. "We were only supposed to bring one person to help!"

Nigel waves the lanyard around his neck. "We were hired by the production company. It's all on the up-and-up."

"WE?"

Nigel points to a dozen robot clones running around the studio. One of the robots, however, doesn't have Nigel's gumball head and is spray-painted neon red and yellow.

"That's not one of mine," Nigel says. "Seems like your competition sees the value in artificial intelligence."

I whip around to watch a shiny robot working alongside Simone and Sam. If their robot is half as smart as they are, I hope Bev, Eric, and I can compete.

My anxiety gets even worse when I realize what Sam and Simone have done for their final project. The LA landmark they chose for their theme is the city's most famous fast-food restaurant: In-N-Out Burger. Their centerpiece is the iconic In-N-Out logo built out of cupcakes and layers of colorful red and yellow origami paper that their robot makes sure is absolutely perfect.

Hundreds of cupcakes in the shape of hamburgers and cheeseburgers line their table. The buns look like they're made out of vanilla cake coated with sesame seeds, the meat is chocolate, and they've used green food coloring on shredded coconut for lettuce. The chocolate-cake patties are frosted with icing that's been colored to look like ketchup and mustard. Simone is putting together trays of French fries that seem to be thin slices of pound cake.

Bev points to Simone's workstation. "I can't believe it. She's making them animal style!"

It's not something they list on their menu, but locals know that at In-N-Out you can order fries "animal style"—topped with grilled onions, melted cheese, and dressing. In Sam and Simone's version, they covered their pound-cake fries with marzipan and crumbled cookies and are even making them extra crispy with their mini-blowtorch.

Bev can't take her eyes off their table. "I don't know how they did it but the room SMELLS like In-N-Out."

"Did Simone make some kind of cheeseburger vapor?" I ask while pressing licorice laces onto our baseball cupcakes. "Everybody's mouth in this place is going to be watering in two seconds!"

"I prefer OUR Burger and Fries." Bev sighs and I know she's thinking about the kittens.

Eric comes back with a big sack of coffee beans. "It's a shame we can't put both tables together. Nothing tastes better at a baseball game than a fresh burger."

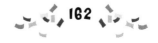

I try to put the finishing touches on our food but it's hard to concentrate when there's so much going on.

I can hear Craig inside my bag asking if I'm okay; he knows how easily I can get over-whelmed. Another cupcake is the LAST thing I want right now, but I open my bag so I can see Craig's smiling face, and that actually takes my stress level down a notch. He's right—Bev and I have been working hard for weeks. Even if we lose to Sam and Simone, we can still be proud of our work in today's finale.

As Craig goes back into hiding, his sprin-kles give me an idea to add some extra pizzazz to our batting cage. I take the magic calculator out of my bag and grab a jar of sprinkles from the baking supplies. When no one's looking, I sneak into our batting cage and dump the sprin-kles into a pile on the floor. Using the calcula-tor, I multiply it until the pile is big enough to stand on.

I wave Bev over. "Voilà, a pitcher's mound!"

"Good thinking!" Bev dives into the giant pile of sprinkles. "You just created the perfect spot for selfies!"

Eric hands us each a cup and tells us he loves the new photo op. "Don't worry—it's hot chocolate, not coffee. Plenty of sugar to get your energy up."

Bev stares into her cup. "You steamed the Dodgers' logo into the foam! Martina, yours is a baseball."

Sure enough, Eric's created a perfectly stitched baseball in the foam of my drink.

Eric raises his cup. "To the winning team."

Christy appears wearing a green, gold, and red striped dress, which from my research I recognize as the city's flag. I wait for her to say something about our stadium or the other team's burger buffet, but she just asks if we need anything before she opens the door to let in the one hundred lucky patrons who will be visiting our exhibits today.

Bev and I exchange glances—we're as ready as we'll ever be.

Christy stands before the doors as the director and Toni adjust the camera. The director counts down on his fingers: three, two, one.

"Hello! Coming to you from *Cupcake Challenge*, I'm Christy Morales." Christy's smile helps me relax a bit more. Our stadium looks terrific and some of our friends from school won a chance to be here today by posting Photoshopped pictures of their faces on cupcakes and tagging *Cupcake Challenge* on Instagram. There's no reason why the next hour won't be a blast.

"Today's theme—if you can't tell by my dazzling dress—is our home city of Los Angeles! Our competitors are locked in a tie. To win today, the challenge wasn't merely to bake a cupcake, but to build an entire cupcake exhibit that captures something about LA that makes it one of the greatest cities in the world. But I can't make this decision by myself. Let's bring in today's guests— who will also be our judges!"

Christy pushes open the double doors to the studio and a hundred cheering fans flood in. It's a pretty awesome feeling to see their faces react to all our hard work. They gasp and point and try to decide which exhibit to visit first.

"BURGERS!" I hear a voice in the crowd that I immediately recognize as Scott's. Bev and I watch him and Mike run to the crowd at Sam and Simone's table.

"You'd think they'd be more interested in baseball," Bev says. "Not to mention the fact that they're our friends."

But within seconds our stadium is also surrounded by hungry fans. Bev works the line, answering questions and posing for photos, while

I supervise the batting cage. I'm only too happy to let Bev be the one to interact with our guests. Not only do I hate posing for photos—especially with kids I don't know—but staying close to the cage allows me to keep an eye on the magic bat.

"Ohhh, I get it," says a girl as I hand her the bat and helmet. "Cupcake batter. Like the batter you use to make cupcakes AND the bat you hit baseballs with. I see what you did there."

I grin and tell the girl she's right. Her father pitches her a cupcake and the girl blasts it to smithereens, sending clumps of frosted cake all over him.

"Great hit, Anna." Her dad wipes a splotch of icing from his glasses. "Maybe a little TOO great."

"Dad's earned a cappuccino." I point them to where Eric is making coffee. I don't know if it's the pressure of being on camera or all the caffeine he's been drinking, but Eric is cranking out drinks faster than I've ever seen him work at the diner.

167

One woman tilts her cup so her son can look at the foam on her cappuccino. "Look, a baseball cap!"

Eric waves me down. "Martina, watch the machine. I'm already low on milk."

Before I can answer, he races out toward the walk-in refrigerator. I set up the next girl to bat some cupcakes into crumbs. She's only a little older than my brother James. I hold out the bat but she frowns and shakes her head.

"I'm not good at sports," she says quietly.

I kneel down and give her a smile. "You'll be great." I put the bat in her hands. "This is a magic bat. There's no way you'll miss."

Suddenly Eric runs up with an armload of milk jugs. "Martina, we've got a situation," he says.

I close my eyes, dreading his next words.

PLEASE can this disaster have nothing to do with my stickers?

TOO HOT to Handle

"One of Nigel's clones freaked out when he saw Simone's kitchen blowtorch," Eric says. "He knocked it out of her hands and the origami sculpture caught on fire."

Before I can race over to help, Eric holds up one of the jugs. "I doused it with milk before it had a chance to spread. You're welcome."

Maybe Eric WAS the best person to bring to the challenge—turns out he's a hero as well as a helper. Or at least until the smoke detector starts blaring.

Eric throws down the empty jugs and runs to the other side of the kitchen. I guess dairy products aren't the best way to put out a fire after all.

I look for Nigel, who's on his headset, keeping people away from Sam and Simone's display, which is smoking and spreading to the other table. Bev runs over and grabs my wrist.

"Maybe your bracelet can still ward off bad things. Use it!"

Bev's belief in the power of stickers has officially exceeded my own. I'd be shocked if the magic bracelet can stop a fire, but I hold out my arm anyway and hope the beads can ward off this disaster.

They don't.

"Stickers can't fix everything," I shout. "We need to help people leave the building."

Several members of the crew run to find fire extinguishers while Christy wonders why the sprinkler system hasn't turned on. I remember what the firefighter who came to our school said last month and guide people toward the exits.

But Christy yelling about the sprinklers makes me realize there is water at my disposal.

The magic bracelet didn't work, but I have a wave!

I find the sheet in my bag and quickly peel off the last sticker, hoping it can help.

whoosh! Poof! Bam!

The wave

explodes into the room, a giant wall of water like the kind people surf in Hawaii. The room is suddenly awash in baseball cupcakes, hamburger cupcakes, and a whole lot of sprinkles. Several of the guest judges body-surf across the room, while some of the younger kids jump off tables into the swirling water.

The good news: the fire is out.

The bad news: everyone is a soggy mess, the studio is damaged, and both our final challenges are ruined.

As if all that isn't bad enough, Nigel and the other androids—including Sam and Simone's—are now in a rusted pile in the middle of the room. The wave that thankfully stopped the fire transformed Nigel and the others into a corroded heap of metal.

While Christy and the crew make sure everyone's okay, I search through the pile of robots for Nigel. When I finally find him, Bev hands me some butter to oil him so he can talk. I feel like Dorothy in *The Wizard of Oz* trying to save the Tin Man.

"I'm sorry!" I tell Nigel. "I was so focused on stopping the fire that I didn't think about how the wave might affect you!"

The gumballs in his head are floating inside the glass and Nigel can barely move his mouth. "I told you stickers could be dangerous," he whispers.

Craig paddles by in a muffin tin, using coffee stirrers for oars. "Nice going, Sticker Girl! For a minute there, I thought we were toast—which is a real downgrade for a cupcake."

There must be drains in the floor of the soundstage because the water quickly subsides. For the first time, Christy doesn't look like she's stepped out of a magazine; with her running mascara and eye shadow she looks like a confused mannequin who just lost a fight with a fire hose. Sam and Simone climb out from their blockade of burgers to assess the damage.

My backpack starts to rumble, which can only mean one thing.

NO! NO! NO!

I open it to find the sheet of stickers is no longer empty. The ant farm, ice cream cone, lipstick, wave, baseball bat, kittens, calculator, and bracelet, as well as Nigel, are back in their assigned slots.

Every sticker except for Craig.

Who shall win?

"All the stickers are going back," I tell Craig. "Are you leaving too?"

He tries to put on a happy face but I can see today took a lot out of him. "I have to," he says. "I'll see you again soon, Martina—I promise."

I lift Craig out of the cup and nuzzle him against my cheek. "Even when things go wrong, it's always great having you here." Before I get to say another word, he's gone—returned to the sheet of stickers.

I wipe the remaining bit of Craig's buttercream

frosting from my cheek. All the stickers are now back on the sheet, safe and sound.

Bev pulls me aside and asks if I'm okay.

I nod yes, but my insides tell me no.

It's only Christy clapping her hands to get our attention that brings my focus back to the room.

"The sprinkler system finally went off!" Bev says. "Everything got soaked!" She gestures to the sprinklers lined up across the ceiling.

Sam and Simone give up trying to rebuild their In-N-Out display and turn their attention to their robot.

Christy takes a deep breath and motions for Toni to start filming.

"You want me to call makeup first?" Toni asks.

"No," Christy replies. "We're keeping it real today."

When Toni's ready, Christy begins. "It seems today's challenge turned into a fight between a fire and our sprinkler system. The question is,

how do we choose today's winner amid all this mess?"

Winning is the last thing on my mind; I just lost my stickers! But Mike and Scott begin chanting, "BOTH TEAMS WIN! BOTH TEAMS WIN!" Soon the entire room joins in.

Christy holds up her hand to quiet the troops. "I suppose it's POSSIBLE that both teams earn a prize—although that's never happened on this show before. But this round of *Cupcake Challenge* seems to be full of firsts."

She looks at one of the producers, who nods and points to the curtain at the back of the room. Has the show's prize been behind there all along?

When Christy pulls back the curtain, we're all shocked to see a cupcake ATM!

Several kids rush to the machine and start ordering cupcakes using the touchscreen.

"That's right," she says. "A Christy's Bakery ATM for your school, your community center, or even your living room if that's where you

want it. Stocked weekly with twelve different flavors of Christy's cupcakes."

Mike and Scott are going bonkers, pressing buttons and planning where in our school the ATM will go. But Bev looks at me and shakes her head. It's nice having someone else besides

Craig know what I'm thinking. Stickers may have gotten me into lots of trouble this year, but they're also one of the reasons Bev and I are BFFs.

"You KNOW where our ATM is going," Bev says.

At the same time we both say, "The diner."

After all this worrying, I might be able to help Dad's business after all.

with sprinkles on top

It turns out Dad's meeting that kept him from coming to the finale went well and his loan was extended so he's as thrilled as we are. Bev and I count the days until the cupcake ATM gets delivered.

When it finally is, we're shocked when the person sent to train us on the new machine is Debbie. She's happy to see us, and it's funny to watch Eric stammer and sweat as she shows us how to use the cupcake ATM. But since he volunteered to help me when I needed it most, I decide not to tease him.

Dad is thrilled to see Debbie, glad about the loan, and excited by the ATM; the only thing holding him back from one hundred percent happiness is how much he misses Nigel. "He didn't even say goodbye," Dad complains. "This place feels empty without him." I tell him the robotics lab was shipped to another school but my explanation barely makes a dent in Dad's sadness. Thankfully the diner is swamped with new customers ordering Christy's famous cupcakes—not in Beverly Hills but right here in the San Fernando Valley. The line at the diner isn't as long as the one at her bakery, but in time, who knows?

While people wait to use the cupcake machine, they also order Dad's dishes and Eric's fancy coffees. He even perfected a foam cupcake he can steam into your latte if you ask him.

Bev heard that Sam and Simone asked their

school if they could install their vending machine on-site so their ATM is outside their cafeteria. Sam covered the entire machine in blue origami paper and Simone rigged up a vapor system so the hallway always smells like fresh-baked cupcakes.

Even after sharing these stories, Bev doesn't complain once that our ATM prize is at the diner, not school. One thing you can say about Bev—she is a VERY good friend.

The *Cupcake Challenge* webisodes finally get posted and I'm both nervous and excited. The comments on the site are mostly positive—thankfully!—noting how hardworking and creative the four of us are. If I had to guess, I'd say Sam and Simone might be the viewers' favorites, so maybe it's a good thing the finale was a tie after all. Seeing all those cupcakes stacked with Craig's buttercream face on our side of the TV kitchen makes me miss him even more.

Ms. Graham gives us less and less homework

as we head toward summer, which is good because Mom, Eric, and I spend every extra minute helping Dad. He keeps saying it's not HIS diner, it's the family business, and it sure is starting to feel that way. Last night Mom was behind the grill with Dad—like when they first met—while Eric and I took turns watching James in between waiting tables. The night was fun-busy, not stressful-busy. Or maybe I'm just getting better at juggling the different parts of my life.

On Saturday, I sit on the back steps and watch James play in his sandbox. His castle is no-where near as good as the kittens' but he's having a great time, which is kind of the point. When he brings out a bat and softball later, I tell him I don't want to play. Without the magic bat, I doubt I'll be able to hit the ball once. But James's enthusiasm is contagious so I pick up the bat and get ready for his pitch.

THWACK!

Even with James's weak throw, I hit the ball straight on, sending it over the fence, just like I did when I used the bat from my sticker sheet.

Who knows? Maybe

has some magic powers of her own.